Thomas Martindale

Sport Royal, I Warrant You!

Twelfth Night

Thomas Martindale

Sport Royal, I Warrant You!
Twelfth Night

ISBN/EAN: 9783337082482

Printed in Europe, USA, Canada, Australia, Japan

Cover: Foto ©Andreas Hilbeck / pixelio.de

More available books at **www.hansebooks.com**

Sport Royal,

I Warrant You!

—Twelfth Night.

THOMAS MARTINDALE

PRICE, ONE DOLLAR.

...Contents

APOLOGETIC.

IF it be true that "good wine needs no bush," it ought to be true that a good book needs no apology. "But," my reader may ask, "is your book a good one, or does its goodness rest only on the modest opinion of its author?" Dear reader, I may safely say, without stretching the bounds of modesty, that any book whose aim is to lengthen and make better the life of the American business man and to show him the most enjoyable way to do it, must be a good book. "But why the American business man rather than another?" Because he is the man whose manner of life affords the broadest room for improvement. He is the man who in his fierce chase after the almighty dollar forgets that there are such things as health and happiness and personal comfort, or if he remembers them it is only to see that they step to the side and not stand in the way of his chase. To stop for rest or recreation would be extravagance, especially as he knows no need of either. A knowledge of the need, however, is sure to come, and when it does he may thank his stars if it hasn't come too late. You cannot teach an old dog new tricks nor can you disentangle the habits of a life time from their worry and care and weave the worn threads into youthful toggery.

Too late! Too late!

I am aware of the dangers that lie in wait for the book-writer. "Oh, that mine adversary had written a book!" was the burden of Job's prayer, 3,500 years ago, and it is doubtful whether the roll of passing centuries has as yet flattened out the peril. Flattering myself, however, that I am no man's adversary, I will take the risk and launch my little volume, hoping for it fair weather, favoring gales, and a broad harbor from which to spread its wholesome freight wherever it may do the most good.   THOS. M.

TO A. B. F. KINNEY.

A FRIEND of thirty years' acquaintance, and the best all-around sportsman I have ever met; a man equally expert with rifle, gun or flyrod; who has killed game of every species that the American Continent affords, from the grizzly bear to the ubiquitous rabbit, from the wild goose and its rival in migratory flight —the mysterious brant—to the solitude-loving woodcock, and who is besides what the world affectionately calls " a royal good fellow." To him this book is respectfully dedicated by his sincere friend,

THOMAS MARTINDALE.

MOOSEHEAD LAKE.

This way lies the game.
– *King Henry VI.*

W E left Philadelphia Saturday night, September 12th, at 6.50, by the Boston express. It was hot, close and miserably uncomfortable. The sleeping car felt like an oven and we turned in before New York was reached, as that was the coolest thing to do. Sunday in Boston was rainy, raw and cold. On Monday morning, in Bangor, we had to put on heavy flannels and get out overcoats.

It was election day in Maine; yet, although it was expected that the Republican ticket would be elected by 30,000 majority, we saw no excitement along the railroad in our ride from Bangor to Greenville, at the head of Moosehead Lake. No bands, no men around the polling places, with badges on. An occasional flag floated in the frosty air but that was all. Yet there was a silent unseen something betokening an enormous Republican vote. (We're in the woods now and have heard nothing of the result as yet.) During our ride in the car a prophetic native sitting behind us broke loose in this fashion: "Darned if I wouldn't bet a dollar that the State would go u-nan-i-mus for Powers, if it weren't for the fac' that some ornery cuss would hear of my bet and go and vote for t'other fellow, just so as I would lose it."

There are a number of little steamboats on Moose-head Lake, which ply backwards and forwards, carrying freight and passengers. Upon a time-card, a sort of "free and easy, go as you please schedule," we were told our boat would leave promptly at six in the morning. So on Tuesday we were up before five o'clock to see to our stores, baggage and hunting outfit being aboard on time, had breakfast in a hurry, first asking the landlord to tell the captain of the boat that we would be aboard at six and not to start without us. At six we were pacing the deck of the steamer, listening to the captain and pilot swearing at the engineer, who had not yet put in an appearance, and the boat couldn't well go without the engineer. Half after six came and we still waited; the whistle was blown repeatedly, but no sign of the man who handled the stop-cocks. At eighteen minutes to seven the "knight of the stopcocks" was seen leisurely coming down a hillside as calmly as if he were an hour ahead of time. Then we made a start and crossed to another landing, where we took in tow a scow with four horses, a party of ladies and some lumbermen. At a quarter to eight we were off for the "Northeast Carry," where we arrived about an hour and a half late, which hour and a half caused us an exciting time.

Northeast Carry is so called because it is a road or "carry" at the northeast end of the lake; it is two miles long, and the other end of the "carry" lands you on the banks of the Penobscot River. As we were loading our canoes a party landed from down the river. In the centre of one of their canoes a lady was seated on a throne-like chair covered with costly Persian rugs.

PENOBSCOT RIVER; LOADING CANOES FOR A TRIP INTO THE WILDERNESS.

Luxurious air cushions supported "my lady's" back, and formed a rest for her feet. An oriental robe, tinted with all the hues of the rainbow, was gracefully thrown around her dainty limbs, mingling its colors with those of the autumn leaves which were strung in garlands about the bow of the boat. A pretty scene indeed, but yet imperfect. It needed a dusky Indian maiden, with no clothes on, to speak of, waving a peacock fan. Then the picture might pass, on a pinch, for that of the proud Cleopatra as she sailed up the Cydnus to tickle the fancy and catch the heart of her love-sick Antony.

Precisely at two o'clock Tuesday, the fifteenth, we paddled away from Northeast Carry. We had a glorious run to the "half-way house," (ten miles down). The river was bewitchingly beautiful. The first frosts had delicately colored the leaves of the maple and beech, while the great waving masses of ferns that fringe the river's edge had changed their greens for various shades of yellow and brown, and spreading their dainty texture along the banks seemed anxious to show what nature could do in the way of embroidery.

Everything looked radiant and happy—save our three guides who were taciturn and troubled. The reason was plain. It was half-past four in the afternoon when we reached the "half-way house." We had stated that we desired particularly to be at Chesuncook Lake (twenty miles down the river) that night, and there would have been no trouble in doing the journey in daylight if the steamer Comet had only been more prompt in starting from Greenville. Now, below us, six miles down, is a great stretch of rapids called the "Rocky Rips," a mile and a half long. Below these rapids come the Pine Stream Falls, half a mile long.

Our three canoes were deeply loaded. Should we or should we not risk the run? It was finally decided to risk it, and away we went, paddling for all we were worth, but it was dark when we reached the head of the "Rips," and we were "in for it."

'Tis a beautiful sight in daylight to see the canoes on these rapids, rushing one after the other from shore to shore, dodging this rock, sliding over that shelf, or doubling around some intruding ledge, all the while striving to keep in the channel, which in some places is not more than four or five feet wide. At night, however, the sight is not quite so captivating, especially if the night be a dark one and you happen to make up a part of the canoe's cargo.

We got through, however, without any greater mishap than breaking the rib of one canoe and shipping some water into another. A few minutes after emerging from the boiling " Rocky Rips " we heard the roar of the falls about a mile further down. The sound was grand, and we thought we were going to have another exciting run, but the guides said that we (the sports) would have to get out, walk through the woods to the bottom of the falls, (about a half mile.) This was to lighten the

PENOBSCOT RIVER: BATEAU ON THE RAPIDS AT "HALF-WAY" HOUSE.

canoes. They then rearranged the loads and started down the falls by water while we went down by land, and it was darker in the woods than it was on the river. We stumbled and tripped over roots and logs, while the guides stumbled and tripped over rocks. We got through all right and so did they—after a fashion. One man had to jump out of his canoe to save it and another man brought his canoe down leaking. Neither man seemed exactly happy. However, there's very little pure happiness in this world and perhaps the adulterated article tastes all the better for its mixture with a little misery.

In a few minutes the loads were changed and we were off again down the river. After a run of about an hour we saw the lights of the Chesuncook House looming up bright and cheery in the distance, and in a little while we stood within its hospitable doors. We found it chock full of guides and "sports," and among the latter was a goodly proportion of "lady sports." No less than four of the "short skirt" variety, who, with their "little" rifles, their "little" boots, their "little" jerseys, their "little" fishing rods and their "little" fellers, made the scene an interesting and we might say (although hanging should be the penalty for such a pun) an amooseing one.

CUPID IN THE WILDERNESS.

This love will undo us all. O, Cupid! Cupid! Cupid!
—*Troilus and Cressida.*

UMAN nature is the same the world over, and Cupid, sly dog that he is, appears to know that the wild woods and lakes and rivers of Maine are no exception to the rule. Ah, me! if these same woods and lakes and rivers had tongues and knew how to use them what queer tales they could tell, and what incidents would come to light that now slide into the past unstoried and unrecorded!

Here, in this very wilderness, hunting, fishing and pleasure parties yearly congregate, and among the latter is plenty of fit food for Cupid's powder. Young and beautiful girls with enough will, skill and ingenuity to paddle their own canoe and make love at the same time— if their chaperones are sleepy enough to permit the performance of such a double barreled programme.

These fishing and pleasure parties remain no longer than the middle or latter part of September, but while they're here the crafty little winged god is up to his chin in business, and to be hit with Cupid's arrow is as common as trouble. Ah,

"Cupid is a knavish lad
Thus to make poor females mad."

But, with all due respect to William Shakespeare I would remind him that it is not from out the female sex alone that Cupid chooses his candidates for the mad-house. The "knavish lad" is no respecter of persons or sex, as the immortal William would soon discover, if his canonized bones could burst their cerements, quit their narrow bed and revisit the glimpses of the moon that overlights this summer habitat of the curly-headed god.

Now I come to think of it, William's bones needn't go to all that trouble. The sad, lamenting tone of the words,

"O, love's bow shoots buck and doe,"

proves that he knew the ambisexability of Cupid's tricks quite as well as he seems to have known everything else.

AN OLD "TOTE" ROAD ALONG THE PENOBSCOT IN EARLY OCTOBER.

Funny indeed are some of the doings and undoings of engaged couples. Here is an instance which I hope the interesting couple with a pair of hearts that "beat as one" will pardon me for giving away. They made the sad discovery that their canoe was too small to hold an embryo bride and her best young man at the same time; but love that "laughs at locksmiths" surely would not cry at a less serious emergency. Its resources are much too ready for that. They placed two canoes side by side, anchored them together with a pair of encircling arms and with a guide to paddle in the stern of each love-laden vessel, went on their way rejoicing.

Now these guides while they know how to paddle know quite as well how to tattle, and tattle, in truth, they do

Of the doings and the wooings,
Of the billings and the cooings,
Of the kissings and the huggings of the pair;
Of the lovings, of the scoldings,
Of the rapturous enfoldings —
Oh, Paradise with lots of fun to spare!

Of course, the guides are only mortals, and as all this takes place within easy reach of their eyes and ears they would be more than mortals—or less—if they didn't tattle. Bless your heart, the amount of it they have retailed to me would more than fill a book the size of Webster's Unabridged. You shall have the benefit of it some day, as I intend to pick out a few of the best, the very best of their stories and print them. Then, oh then, look out for something rich, rare and racy; but not now. We'll first give these turtle doves a chance to get married.

A new crowd of visitors have appeared in the Maine woods and waters. Visitors who are bent on killing the succulent deer, the solitude-loving caribou and the lordly moose (the noblest Roman of them all.)

The visitors, by the force of circumstances, are obliged to have guides whose particular policy it is to "speed the parting 'sport' and welcome the coming one." In the various places where these guides meet, Greenville, Kineo, Northeast Carry, Chesuncook House, Mud Carry, Eagle Lake or Churchill Lake and hundreds of other places, there's a great comparing of notes of the many things said and the many things done by the departed guests. As I have already hinted, I may at some future time give you the pith of a few of these notes.

It is surprising how many Philadelphians there are already in the woods for the fall hunting, which started October 1st, and how many more we hear of that are coming. Every hotel register is well sprinkled with names of residents of our Quaker City, more, I think, than from any other place. One of my guides hurt his knee, so that the limb swelled to double its natural size. I was considering how I could send him home (a journey by canoe, of over five days, which with five more days, for the return of the guide who took him out, made the matter a very serious one). He relieved my mind, however, by telling me he had heard of a doctor who was camped at the head of a bog a few miles away. I put my man at once into a canoe and paddled up to the tent of the Esculapian disciple whom I found to be an eminent one and a Philadelphian. After looking at the man's damaged limb, he said: "Well, I am an expert, or considered so, on insanity, and perhaps on one or two other of nature's calamities, but I am not an expert on swelled legs. However, this is what I advise you to do." And he told him. The doctor's advice seems to have been—what a doctor's advice sometimes is not—the proper thing, for the leg got well. But before the man could call again to return his thanks and tell the good doctor of the cure, that individual had vanished further into the wilderness, and I've not seen him since.

PENOBSCOT RIVER WITH ITS FIRST COAT OF ICE; OCTOBER 19TH, 1895.

The natives hereabout are, in money matters, what the Scotch call "canny." And canny enough some of them are, to give any Scotchman points and beat him with ease. Listen to this. A storekeeper, "a native here and to the manner born," had a mother. I don't wish you to infer, however, that he differed in this particular from any other storekeeper. He was a dutiful son, and doted on his mother, showing her every mark of filial affection. This was, of course, very commendable in him, but she deserved it all, for report says she was a "grand woman." In the course of human events, the old lady became "worrited." Life's cares and troubles came so thick and fast they began to choke up the oil in her lamp of life. It commenced to flicker and grow dim and needed only a puff of apoplexy to put it out entirely. When the end came the son's grief was touching, and the more so as there was no place he could obtain a coffin nearer than a town three days' journey away. How to get there and back in time to bury the old lady decently troubled his mind, and the indecency of burying her in one of their common pine receptacles was more shocking to his delicate sense of propriety than planting her in a dry goods box. At this juncture a man who had long known and revered the departed woman volunteered his services to fetch a coffin. With sturdy strokes of his paddle in the "dead" waters of the river and the deft use of the pole in pushing up over the "quick" waters he hurried on. After reaching a "carry" he almost ran across it (two miles) to catch the first boat to the town where coffins were for sale, made his purchase and speeded back to the "carry." Putting the coffin in his canoe he started down the river as rapidly as elbow grease and paddle could drive him. When he landed, the son of the deceased asked him what his charge would be for the trip. The man replied that he would make no charge, that the deceased had always been kind to him, and what he had done was little enough to show the good will and respect he had for her, and that he was glad to have been able to make the trip as he had done. "But" he said, "I wouldn't mind having a plug of tobacco; mine was all used up on the trip." The dutiful son handed him a plug from behind the counter and in the most kind-hearted tone said: "Ten cents, please." This he said and nothing more.

CALLING THE MOOSE.

Sport Royal, I warrant you.'

Twelfth Night.

IN the latter days of September and the early weeks
of October the mammoth deer known as the moose is
mating. Then it is that the woods of Maine, Nova
Scotia and New Brunswick are traversed by thousands
of sportsmen with their guides all in search of one thing
—a chance to kill a bull-moose. Now the female moose,
in one particular, is very like some other females of the
animal kingdom; she is coy and capricious, leading her
lover "a merry dance o'er moss and fell," through bog
and swamp, along the margins of lakes and ponds and
lagoons or "logans" as the latter are called in this
region. At night she comes down to the water to feed
on the roots and tops of the lily pad which grows so
abundantly in sluggish waters. If her mate be her
escort, he usually stands on the bank, eyeing his spouse
tenderly as she feeds, and, with ears cocked, is ever ready
to protect her from all danger, real or fancied.

If the bull moose has no cow of his own but is
merely ranging and scouring the country to find a sweet-
heart that suits his fancy, then is the time he is apt to fall
into a trap and a very sure one. On a still night (and,
mind you, the night must be still) around every lake,
pond and river where the moose frequents and feeds, the

bull hears the sounds of sweetest melody; sounds filled with such plaintive, loving, caressing, lonely, forsaken, "come-to-my-arms" sort of cadence that he cannot resist the appeals. These loving sounds, termed the "call" with their ascending and descending notes are produced by the guides, their instrument being a birch bark horn. If the "call" be well made it will be heard by the bull miles and miles away. Pricking up his ears he will start on the run, thrashing through the brake, barking, bellowing, grunting and in his own affectionate manner answering the impassioned notes of his counterfeit mistress. When he reaches the edge of the wood he grows wary and suspicions. He will steal up and down among the bushes listening and scenting in a "she-may-be-fooling-me" sort of way, and sometimes it takes many nights to convince him that he is the identical gentleman the lady moose is "stuck on," and for whom she is so lovingly calling. Alas, how many a bull-moose Lothario falls a victim to his own vanity and the bewitching notes of a birch bark horn!

Although the bull-moose is a thoroughbred Mormon, having sometimes as many as five wives in his harem, yet when he has one of them specially under his protection he will hardly leave a bird in hand for one in the bush. I have myself heard him answer a "call" while engaged in his protective duty, and then make a start, which in this instance was for two miles; but the loving voice of the real moose called the wanderer back to his protectorate duties and the family bosom. I heard and saw all this. Saw him approach the water, step into it and splash it with his feet, meanwhile looking cautiously around as if he scented danger. And there was danger and a good deal of it in the air. In the front of a canoe sat a hunter—one of the "sports,"—with rifle ready cocked, and heart throbbing and thumping as though it would burst the buttons off his coat. A moment of hold-your-breath suspense, and then bang! goes the 45-90 cartridge, the report sounding and resounding through the woods and over the waters for miles around. There was another bang and yet another, but whether it was the uncertain light or the excitement which interfered with the hunter's aim, or whether it was due to his sitting for hours "still as a mouse" and in an atmosphere with the thermometer at freezing point, I can't say. But I can say that the moose escaped unharmed, untouched by the bullet that might have forever put an end to his Mormon habits and Don Juanish journeys.

The sport of moose hunting is one that requires a great deal of patience and perseverance under such trying difficulties as exposure to cold and loss of sleep. But your reward is ample—plenty of excitement, and if successful, a magnificent antlered head as a trophy of your prowess.

Last night my guide and I set out to paddle up the inlet of a little lake we are encamped upon, with the intention of "calling" if it should be still enough to do so. There was some wind on the lake, but we thought there might be little or none in the forest-sheltered inlet. I was tucked down in the front of the canoe with blankets, to keep my legs warm (for it is cold, very cold, up here), with heavy woolen socks drawn over my boots and a woolen cap down over my ears. We paddled about a mile and found the wind worse than it was on the lake below, and so strong as to make it hard canoeing. In a big bog on the right-hand side we heard a branch break. We stopped and listened. A deer, we both thought, as another and another branch broke. Then came the sound of heavy footfalls and we knew a moose was "coming to the water." We listened intently, so intently that I could hear the ticking of my watch, though it was buried under a sweater, a coat and an overcoat; nay, more, I heard—perhaps it may have been fancy—the stretching of my elastic suspenders as I breathed. Soon we distinguished through the dark of the moonless night a great object, big as a hippopotamus, move down the bank and step into the water. The guide pushed the canoe up deftly and silently, but the wind was at its worst at this time and blew the canoe diagonally against a tree top sticking out of the water on the other shore. This made a noise, little it is true, but yet it sounded, oh, how great! Just then we saw another huge object on the bank. Now, up to this time, we could not make out whether the monster in the water was a bull or a cow-moose (and it was rather important to know which, as a fine of $100 and three months imprisonment is the penalty imposed for shooting a cow.)

It was so dark I couldn't see whether the big object had horns or not; but the guide settled the problem with " be quick ! that's him on the bank—now down him !" I raised my rifle, aimed for what I believed to be his shoulder, and pulled the trigger, but, horror of horrors, the hammer wouldn't budge; again I sighted and pulled, and yet again, but all to no purpose. My rifle was more harmless than a pocket pistol loaded with Jersey applejack. The cow soon took alarm, floundered up the bank and in the twinkling of an eye they were both gone, he bellowing and barking through the alders, crashing down everything before him in his mad rage and fury, and she silently stealing away in the darkness and seclusion.

There were two very disgusted men that night—one because the other didn't shoot and the other because his rifle wouldn't shoot. On coming into camp I made an examination of the trouble and found that on account of several days' steady rain the lock of the rifle had become so rusty (although greased every day) that it would not work, and thereby the life of a bull-moose was probably saved. A job also awaits a gunsmith, if one can be found, capable of taking a rifle apart and fixing it so that it will obey the trigger, at least one time out of three.

We have now been in the woods in the northern part of Maine for over three weeks. In that time, I think, we've had but two fine days, the rest being made up of wind, rain, snow and ice; winds from all points of the compass; winds strong, to the strength of a gale, then softening down to a zephyr, but still they were winds; cold winds, warm winds, moist winds, dry winds (you see we're "moose calling," and you cannot call moose successfully in windy weather; that is the reason we notice the wind). Rains? Yes, of all degrees and conditions; soft rains and hard rains, gentle rains and furious downpours—one of which is now having things its own way as I write this. My guides are building a break-rain, break-weather, break-water (or whatever you may please to call it) of fir trees. They are planning where to put the "door," but as the rain seems to blow from every-where, it will probable result in carrying the fir grove clear around the camp.

During this miserable rainy spell I have watched the game with some interest (what little of it I've been able to see) to learn how they relish the damp humor of Jupiter Pluvius. They seem to fancy it no more than do their enemies the human bipeds.

Yesterday I observed some partridges huddled under a big log, with feathers wet and all their glory of color and fluffy sleekness departed. The cock bird looked woe-begone and cheap and ragged—a dripping melancholy shadow and I thought of the poet's lament:

> "Shades of the mighty can it be
> That this all remains of thee?"

To-day I started a deer from out of a clump of young pines, where he had been sheltering himself. Again I came across an old doe standing under a couple of big cedar trees, and after she had "lit out" I went and sat down in her "arbor." Although the rain was coming down in streams, yet none fell on me and I spent there a couple of happy hours watching the capers of the only living things that had the courage to brave the storm— the red squirrels. They were busily occupied in laying up their winter stores which seemingly were to consist of pine cones, as each had one of these in his mouth. I noticed, though, they took good care to run along the ground under the logs, and not on top of them.

We take the weather philosophically, because we're well prepared for it, having plenty of dry clothes, a big camp to come to, a roaring fire, an abundance of the finest game in the world to eat, clear spring water (a mineral spring at that) to drink, good appetites and rugged strength to go out upon a big tramp every day, no matter whether the weather is what it ought to be or whether it isn't.

It is asserted that at least fifteen hundred sportsmen are now in the Maine woods. If so, there'll be fully two thousand guides, making an army of say three thousand five hundred people, many of them with only a week or ten days' time at their disposal, and some of them accompanied by ladies. So, while it is bad for us it is much worse for "the other fellers," whose short supply of time won't allow them to wait for the glad sunshine to come. Why, therefore should we complain?

AN UNEXPECTED TREAT.

Who comes here? My doe?
—*Merry Wives.*

A COUPLE of evenings since we had a quiet spell for a few hours, and my guide and I started out moose "calling." We pushed our canoe very cautiously up the inlet of the little lake we're camped on, paddling as lightly as possible, stopping frequently to listen, peering with expectant eyes into every bunch of alders, every clump of young pines, hoping against hope that we might see a moose "coming to water." It was about five in the afternoon, and the scenery along the brook was clothed in beauty beyond the poets fancy or the painter's palet e. The brown and green tints of the frosted and unfrosted ferns ; the tufts of waving grasses with their green blades tipped with yellow ; the alders just beginning to put on their autumn brown ; the red maple, the yellow birch, the dark green pines, the stately juniper, the sad cypress, and all mirrored in the tawny stream that flowed lazily beneath, without a ripple to disturb or fret the reigning silence.

Silence ? Yes ! Nature seemed to be up to her neck in the depths of the hush as the guide shoved our canoe on a pine root to anchor it. After he did so, he took up his birch bark horn and gave the three "calls" of the cow-moose. First, the short, tremulous wail ; then the more urgent and commanding one, and, lastly, the long, resonant, loving, coaxing, beseeching appeal, which no living bull-moose with any bowels of compassion can resist. To produce this call the guide winds the horn around in continued circles, the motion giving the sound that trembling, undulating effect which the genuine article always has.

Immediately after the "call" we heard a branch break in the woods to the right of us, a hundred yards, perhaps, away. I took up my field-glass and watched until I saw a couple of bewitching eyes, a pair of ears, erect and vigilant, and the peculiarly graceful neck which I knew could belong only to the doe deer. She stood between two cedars and for a while watched us intently, then stole carefully up the stream to where it turned sharp to the left and where a bank covered with marsh grass made a pretty foreground for the picture. Here she planted herself, rigid, with nostrils dilated, ears standing straight up, eyes fixed on us, and with every other indication that we were the only object that at present occupied her attention and curiosity. The guide gave the moose "calls" every few minutes and they could be heard miles away, yet there she stood, truly, "a thing of beauty" if not a joy forever.

The day waned, the sun sank behind a mass of clouds, twilight came and went, still there she stood, motionless, entranced, bewitched silhouetted against the evening sky like a graceful statue. And when the cloak of night shut us from her sight then her curiosity seemed to become uncontrollable. We could not see, but heard her cross the brook softly, then steal down the left bank picking her way daintily behind the alders and cedar trees until she was abreast of us. A few minutes of silence and we could almost imagine her letting loose her curiosity : " Who can these mortals be? Are they living creatures? And what heavenly music that was! Poor things, how can they sit so long on the water and keep so still! And what are they after anyway?" She no doubt thought all this if she didn't say it. Then she stepped out in the open and came so close to the canoe we could almost have hit her with a paddle. Did we shoot! No, sir! No thought had we of killing that trusting, unsuspecting creature, whose beauty and grace of form and pose had for an hour entranced our sense with a vision of loveliness we can never forget. Venison? Why we would have gone without the dainty dish for many a day rather than have gotten it by the foul murder of that gentle, soft-eyed, gazelle-like doe of Chesuncook Lake.

KILLING THE CARIBOU.

WE had been semi-prisoners for about three weeks, with rains and high winds, which effectually prevented the hunting of big game successfully in the location of our camp. Early on the morning of Monday, October 5th, my guide said to me " suppose we go and try to hunt that dam." We had heard a great many stories about a dam at the head of the stream which forms the inlet to our little lake but were inclined to think some of these stories Munchausenish. None of our guides had ever seen the dam and had only hearsay for its location and distance. One maintained it was but five miles away; another six, and the third one vowed it was a good eight miles off; besides there are two branches to the stream, and no one knew on which branch the dam was placed. So the guide and I started in light hunting order, with a few bouillon capsules which were to serve us for dinner and supper and possibly breakfast, if we shouldn't get back that night. We found a " spotted " path through the woods that led to an old " tote " road up which we went splashing through the water accumulated by weeks of rain ; up to our very knees in mud sometimes, slipping, falling and stumbling over cedar roots, climbing over and under windfalls, until we reached an old lumber camp, which the guide went down to investigate. No Maine guide can pass an old camp for the first time without having a "look in" to see if anything's been left that he can make use of. Before he reached the buildings three deer, one of them a big buck, jumped out of some raspberry bushes, and bounded away over the creek and into the woods beyond.

I started for them and stalked them for nearly an hour, until I came within shooting distance of the does; but although I heard the buck I could not get my eyes upon him, and the does I did not want; so I returned to the road. We now had a journey of three and a half miles over a road probably as bad as could be found anywhere; that is, if mud, water, alders, alder roots, cedar roots, windfalls and slippery rocks could make it so. There's an end to all things, however, and the road finally led us to a "landing" on the brook where a large number of logs were left high and dry from the last drive. Some of them, in fact, looked as if they had been there for years. There were probably half a million feet in and near this spot We crossed the brook and found a logging road, which we followed for a mile or more, but no signs of a dam. We heard an occasional deer cracking a dry limb in the dense wood or thicket of small pines, which bordered the roadway on either side, but couldn't get a sight of them. Here the guide said we'd better turn back, as we were going in the wrong direction, but I proposed walking at any rate half a mile further, and probably we might find something worth shooting at. We made one turn in the road when we heard a branch break in front of us. We stopped to listen, and soon a calf caribou came out from the right hand side.

It looked up and down, saw us, but moved into the forest on the other side (which was here open and filled with stunted spruce trees, growing in a thick bed of moss). The calf was followed a minute later by a cow. The guide whispered, "now look out for horns." But still another cow came out and crossed the road, followed by a sight I shall never forget. A pair of monster antlers were very slowly pushed out into the road, and after them the head and neck of as grand a caribou bull as sun ever shone upon. It was fully a second later before the animal came into full view.

The guide whispers, "Hit him in the shoulder; be steady and sure." And I was sure, for when I fired my 45-90 rifle almost at the same instant the caribou dropped in his tracks. He hadn't moved an inch after being hit. The ball had passed through his left shoulder and out at the neck. We soon covered the hundred yards or more of distance which separated us from his lordship, whom we found down on his knees unable to rise. And then a battle royal started between Lou Barnes, the guide, and the bull. Barnes wanted to finish him with the back of the ax, and in order to do so, he would angle around him, trying to get in a blow on the forehead. The caribou, however, although unable to raise himself to his feet, could, and did, swing his great head and antlers around in every direction with vicious and lightning-like movement. Had he caught the guide with his "frontlets" or antlers it would have been a sorry day for that individual. Another shot from my rifle, however, settled the matter.

THE "SPORT" AND HIS NOBLE PRIZE.

We then elevated his head and shoulders upon some skids, that were in the road, so as to keep him in good shape, and then tramped back to our camp, a walk of fully six miles. Next day, our three guides, my son and I went back, taking a camera with us, and, although the morning was rainy and squally, we obtained a fairly good picture of him. As he was frozen pretty stiff, the men raised him up on his feet, and, fastening a rope from each antler to a couple of trees on both sides of the road (so as to hold his head up, and thus steady the whole carcass), the photographer (my young son) was enabled to take him in a standing position.

The guides skinned him, taking his head off unskinned. The next day, in order to incur no risk of having the head spoiled by the wet weather or careless skinning, I sent a guide with it to Greenville (a three days' journey there and back. The bull was fourteen years old. The antlers are thirty-two inches long from the base of skull to the tips, and have thirteen points on each side.

The taxidermist to whom the head was sent said it was the finest he had ever seen and the largest he had any record of. On the night of the fifth of October, although very tired and badly used up with our frightfully hard walk, neither the guide (Barnes) nor I slept much. The caribou would haunt our sleep. We could see him almost every minute of the night and even now the memory of the scene is as fresh and vivid as it was on that day, and I am sure will be for many moons to come.

MORE OF THE MOOSE.

The Paragon of Animals.
—*Hamlet.*

THE same morning of the caribou hunt, we left the old bull lying in the road, and started back upon our tracks, at about eleven o'clock, to prosecute our search for the dam we had originally started out to find. Upon reaching the brook we followed it upward some distance, until the guide, who was quite "done up," said he'd make a fire and boil some hot water in a tin dipper for my dinner. I decided, however, to push on until I found that dam, telling him to stay where he was until my return.

BARNES, THE GUIDE, " DONE UP " ON A CARIBOU HUNT,
DRAWS COMFORT FROM HIS PIPE.

The stream here was choked up with cut logs, which made it nice and easy walking, or easy jumping from log to log. Twenty minutes of this sort of travel and I reached the long-looked-for dam.

Climbing on top of it my eye caught the view of as lovely a spot for big game to feed in as could well be imagined. The water had been drawn off during the late spring, and a luxurious growth of swale grass, cranberry bushes and young alder shoots had sprung up in wild and wanton profusion.

I sat me down on the dam and let my senses wallow in the sight. A stiff breeze was blowing, swaying the tall grasses into waves of graceful motion and bringing to my ear a gentle rustling sound—a twittering *pianissimo*, as it were, in one of Nature's *pastorales*, and which all lovers of her rural melodies will recognize and appreciate.

After my fancy had played awhile it ran up against the thought: " What a tempting sanctuary is this for big game! Surely it won't be long without its antlered heads and arched necks." Instinctively, I crept behind some bushes and watched and waited. Fifteen or twenty minutes passed and without my expectations being filled. Then I thought of my tin cup of bouillon, and, fearing it would be spoiled, reluctantly left the enticing spot and traveled back over the logs to where the guide was waiting for me.

After drinking my bouillon I told the guide how near the dam was; what a wonderfully attractive spot for game it must be, told him to take my rifle and go up and look at some big moose tracks that I had found, and I would boil another cup of water for his dinner while he was gone. The fire had burned down low. I put on more wood and sat and watched the roaring blaze, and whistled while supreme contentment oozed out of me from every pore.   My reverie lasted till broken by Barnes, who rushed in with hardly enough wind left to shape his words.   He told me that just as he got to the dam a young bull-moose, with a monstrously big cow-moose, had come out of the woods and were feeding in the open close to the dam.   It didn't take long for us to get back to that dam.   We jumped like gymnasts across the logs and made some leaps that might have caused the kangaroo to blush and hide her head in her pouch.

We approached the dam itself, however, very carefully, and peered over the edge of it to the open space beyond.   The bull was not in sight and the cow was more than five hundred yards away.   They, no doubt, had scented the smoke from our fire, although the wind was very nearly directly in our favor.   But we soon saw that the cow was uneasy and suspicious.   She would raise her mane up and then elevate her head in the air, holding it there for a minute or so, and then start feeding again.   This she did three times, and then she gave a call that was almost instantly answered by the bull, who came rushing out of the woods to the back and to the right of her, as she ran to meet him.   Then they wheeled about, threw up their great heads, and with dilating nostrils, both sniffed the suspicious scent which had alarmed the cow so much.   They were at this moment fully six to seven hundred yards off, and would soon make a dash for the woods, for every moment seemed to increase their alarm.

I said to Barnes: "What do you think about it? Can I down that bull at this distance?"

"I don't think you can, but there's no telling what a 45-90 rifle can do. If you're going to try it you'd better begin, as they'll soon be off."

I decided to try the shot, and still keeping under the edge of the dam, I fired, aiming for the bull's shoulder. My shot was a clean miss. Then we saw a scene that illustrated the amount of human nature that underlies the instinct of the moose. As the report of the rifle rang out and echoed around the edges of the forest encircling the open space, the cow-moose ran here and there in every direction, as if fear had entirely dethroned her courage and prudence. But the bull stood still, rigid, erect, his mane up, while every hair on his body bristled defiance.

I fired cartridge No. 2, making another miss, and a repetition of the scene just described followed, the bull standing still as ever. I reasoned that the strong quartering wind to the right was deflecting the bullets, so I aimed a third time a little more to the left, and fired.

You should have seen the sight that followed. The bullet had struck the bull and he started with a rush and a crash like a locomotive off the rails. Away he went, straight for the woods to the left. The guide and I then sprang upon the top of the dam and watched the cow who was still running about in the open, thoroughly panic-struck. A couple of minutes elapsed and then the bull, although wounded, ran back out of his stronghold of timber to get the cow in out of danger. This gave me a chance to fire three more shots at him. While he was circling around the cow to lead her into the safe seclusion of the woods, he seemed to say: "You can shoot at me all you like, and kill me if you can, but I'll save my frou or perish in the attempt!"

And just as soon as she was headed and started right, then he got away also, both entering the woods to the left.

And then the question was: What shall we do? Barnes said: "Let's go back to camp and give him a chance to lie down. If he's mortally wounded we'll find him, but I fear you've given him only a flesh wound." We stopped at our fire for Barnes to drink his bouillon which now was cold, and then commenced our eight-mile journey to our tent. On the road down, before we reached the logging camp, where we had started the buck deer and the two does the day before, I crept along very cautiously, hoping to catch a sight of the big buck. The road that led by the old camp had a path in which were several long logs leading lengthwise from the road right to the camp, and walking on these logs with rubber boots made no noise at all. Suddenly I came upon no less than six deer feeding in and around a lot of raspberry bushes. Four of them were so bunched at one time I could have placed a bullet that would have gone, possibly through four of them, certainly through three. But they were all does; the buck wasn't there and I stole back to the "tote" road without even alarming them.

It was dark when we reached camp. We were tired, very tired. The excitement of the day had been so great that neither guide nor "sport" could sleep. The caribou, and the moose, and the six deer kept marching in procession through our mind, followed by the queries: "Will we find the moose? Is he killed? Will anything get at the caribou during the night and mutilate him?" In our mind's eye we saw the old fellow dropping in his tracks, saw the bull-moose rushing from the woods to coax the wife of his bosom back from the reach of bullets and into a place of safety.

And thus the day's adventures would re-enact themselves with vividness and over and over again till daylight broke. Then ready and eager to solve our caribou queries, if they were solvable, all the guides (three), my son and myself had breakfast, shouldered camera, axes, rifles and ropes and started off with the intention first to photograph and skin the caribou and secure his head and then to trail the wounded moose. It was half-past one when we reached the dam, and in a few minutes we found the trail of the bull by discovering a pool of blood in the swale grass and another considerable pool on the edge of the woods. After that the trail of the cow-moose and the bull were so intermixed that it was hard to unravel them. But there were five of us, and each would every minute or two discover a trace, a splash of blood on the side of a tree, or a drop on a leaf, or a streak of it on some deadfall the wounded moose had stepped over. At one place he had passed between two trees, which had been a tight fit, as it showed the blood from where he was struck (on the left hip) down his leg as far as the knee. At another place he had stopped and quite a circle of blood was formed. But nowhere was there any sign that he had lain down. Nowhere was there blood enough to show that he had been mortally hit. We followed his trail for over two hours and then reluctantly concluded that our moose would live and prosper perhaps for many a year to come, as he would always in future be duly careful to keep as far away from the range of a rifle as his haunts and habits would permit, and he would never, never again feed in a meadow in daylight during the open season, for a moose only needs to be shot at once to make him forever after the most careful animal that roams the wild, wild woods.

THE GREAT NORTHWEST

Well hast thou lesson'd us.

—*Titus Andronicus.*

THE first thing that struck my attention on my trip, was Canada's nagging policy in regard to American travel.

I had two guns and a case of shells on which duty was claimed. These, I explained, had been in use over six years, and that I was only going to shoot a few days in Canada and then would return with them across the borders, but my explanation had no weight. The shells were counted and duty at the rate of 35 per cent. exacted upon them, with conditions that if I took the guns back out of Canada within two months they would refund the duty, but not if they should be kept a day over that limit. Such is international courtesy between two countries with a border line of four thousand miles.

I passed through the famous "Soo" Canal, where our Government is enforcing its "retaliation policy" against Canada. It was therefore interesting to hear the conversations of the Canadians and Americans on the vessel and along the canal. We were detained there four hours in getting an entrance to the lock. The Canadians point out the fact that their own canal, which is now in course of construction, will be finished in two years, and then will come their time to retaliate by putting up the tolls to American vessels in the Welland and other Canadian water-ways. They say it was a small, petty thing for a great country like the United States to do, and that Canada will more than get even in the long run.

The Americans, on the other hand, say it serves the Canadians right, for they are always nagging and bullying us behind England on the fisheries, the Behring Sea and other questions, and it is time to teach them a lesson. The commerce passing through this canal in Canadian bottoms is very small, last year being only a little over 4 per cent. of the whole. Out of an almost continuous procession of steamers, tugs and sailing vessels which we passed in the "Soo" River only one was Canadian, and she was a small fishing smack. So, pecuniarily, the retaliation policy doesn't amount to much; it is the sting and smart of it that counts. American craft go through free and Canadian craft pay 20 cents per ton toll.

It is said that more tonnage passes through the "Soo" Canal than through the famous Suez Canal. The "Soo" Canal is open only about seven months in the year, and it is totally inadequate for the immense traffic passing through it; therefore our Government is building a new canal, with a lock 800 feet long, 80 feet wide and 21 feet deep. The present lock is 515 feet in length, with a 60 foot entrance, 80 foot inside and about 14 foot 6 in depth. The Canadian Government is making theirs 1000 feet long and 60 feet wide throughout, but if they do not put on an increased force of workmen it will be five years before it can be completed. The United States Canal is reasonably sure of completion within two years.

There is no object lesson equal to this canal for demonstrating the enormous resources of the great Northwest. As far as the eye could reach in both directions was an unending procession of vessels bound both up the lakes and down; those passing down being loaded to the deep water line with iron ore, grain, lumber, etc.; those passing up, with coal and general merchandise. And so it is every day while navigation is open.

What a lot of people with diversified pursuits our Canadian Pacific steamer was carrying! Sitting opposite to me at table was a typical Englishman, formerly a coffee planter in Ceylon, but now a large land proprietor in Manitoba. Another Englishman had been out to the East Indies elephant shooting, and was on his way to the Rocky Mountains to try his hand on the grizzly bear. He was a strenuous advocate of the Martini-Henry rifle for large game, and wouldn't think of shooting a Winchester (probably because it is American). A number of passengers were going to shoot prairie chickens, ducks, etc., others were on their way to buy land near Winnipeg. One wanted to sell land up there, and wanted to sell it badly. Merchants were returning from England, Montreal and Toronto, having bought their fall and winter stock; others were journeying across the continent en route to Japan and China.

Coming up the "Soo" (or Sault Ste Marie) River, out of Georgian Bay, on Sunday last, I was profoundly impressed with the magnitude of the resources of the great Northwest. An almost continuous string of grain or ore laden schooners, steamers, barges and "whalebacks" kept passing us for miles and miles, and on arriving at the mouth of the canal, which is but a mile long, we were detained five hours waiting our turn to get through its one lock. The vessel in front of us was the largest steamer on the lakes—the Mariposa—over 4000 tons burthen, and while the lock comfortably accommodated four large schooners at one lockage, this steamer just about filled the lock, so that no other vessel could enter. She belonged to Ashtabula, O., and was going up with a light cargo of coal and would load iron ore for her return trip. The Canadians seem to think that our Government made a mistake in enforcing the retaliation policy on this canal but don't care very much about it, now that the astonishment and surprise at the action have worn away. The Canadian Pacific Railway is the principal and about the only sufferer, and they cannot be very severely hit, as the total Canadian tonnage passing through the canal last year was, as I have said, but a fraction over 4 per cent. of the whole.

On reaching Fort William (an old Hudson Bay Company's fort), the very first thing to attract my notice was a big wagon load of fine French clarets, brandies and Canadian whiskies, marked ''Hudson Bay Company.'' I know not how strong the proof of the liquors may have been, but I do know that the load itself was to me proof strong as Holy Writ, that the people up this way have expensive tastes and the wherewithal to gratify them. From an unusually intelligent and well informed commercial traveler, Robert Atkinson, of London, Canada, I learned that the head offices of the Hudson Bay Company for this district are at Winnipeg, and that on his last trip to that town there were no less than thirty-two drummers at the principal hotel; that these represented the dry goods and ready-made clothing interests alone, and that the buyers for these departments of the Hudson Bay Company looked at every man's samples before they bought a dollar's worth. Now, as this company also sells groceries, wines, crockery, hardware, drugs, stoves and tinware, guns, ammunition, etc., the reader will easily see what an enormous trade they still monopolize up here.

At Fort William the C. P. R. R. has three big grain elevators, which at the present time are full to the roof, and yet they are shipping by lake and through the canal as fast as they can get boats loaded. The capacity of these elevators are 1,250,000 bushels. The train we met at Fort William was the trans-continental express. It had eleven cars, two of which were filled with Chinese passengers ticketed through from New York to China. Two cars of colonists were going out to settle at different points on the line. The cars were clean and comfortable-looking, and were used at night as sleepers, having the same arrangement as to berths as the Pullmans, without, of course, the luxurious appointments which characterize the latter. There is but one through train a day, and this averages about twenty-two miles an hour.

The road is a single track, well ballasted, has splendid rolling stock and good motive power. I am informed that the management of the line contemplates bestowing the same attentions on the through first-class passengers as the trans-Atlantic steamship companies do, such as passing fresh fruit, beef tea, lemonade, etc., around to the passengers frequently during the day. This will be an innovation that other lines would do well to follow. The Michigan Central already has commenced to present bouquets of flowers to passengers on reaching a certain station. Such little attentions do not cost much and they make a good advertisement.

The city of Winnipeg, with a population of 25,000, was a veritable surprise to me. It has broad streets, half as wide again as our Market Street, four lines of street car tracks, electric lights, electric railways, opera house (with Margaret Mather now playing there), fine stores, and a hotel that would put to shame any we have in Philadelphia. It has a frontage on the main street of 216 feet, is seven stories high, with a rotunda forty by ninety feet, a dining-hall fifty feet wide, ninety feet long and twenty-six feet high, grandly lighted by three copper electroliers, aided by a blaze of wall fixtures. Then there are massive stone fire-places and also a balcony at one end, where an orchestra enlivens the dinner hour.

The hotel has turkish and ordinary baths, private supper and dining-rooms, is heated by steam and lighted throughout by an elaborate electric plant. The charges are from $3 to $7 per day, and the hotel is well supported. This hotel, this city, this Canadian Pacific Railroad, with its progressive management, are indexes of the enterprise of the Canadian Northwest. Here the "star of empire may well hold its sway:" here future provinces and cities will rise from the level table land of the prairies, by the limpid waters of the Assiniboine and Red Rivers, and become rich, prosperous and happy in the lavish and generous returns from the tillage of the fruitful soil. Future colonies will leave their mother country, where the "dry husks of poverty" are their support to find here a glorious paradise of plenty. Here will grow up a strong-lunged, magnetic generation, which must wield a beneficent influence upon the rest of Canada, and why not upon sections of our own country that must surely come in contact with its almost boundless agricultural wealth and resources?

As we were about leaving Winnipeg yesterday, a banker of that lively town, in speaking of the boundless expanse of rich wheat lands around Winnipeg, said: " While the land in the neighborhood of Winnipeg raises fine wheat and lots of it, one thousand miles further north they raise just as much wheat to the acre and just as good." One thousand miles further north. Think of it! I do not know and could not find out in what latitude Winnipeg is situated. I asked the clerk at the Manitoba House, among others. He said he really couldn't tell, but one thing sure, it is an awful cold latitude. The railway guide says it is one thousand four hundred and twenty-four miles from Montreal, and yet good lands are being cultivated a thousand miles still further north. This fact helps to explain the enormous quantities of freight the Canadian Pacific Railroad is sending down, both by rail and water, to the lakes and through the St. Lawrence River.

At Regina, the capital of the province of Assiniboia, we were much interested in the House of Parliament, the Governor's Mansion and the barracks and drill ground of the famous mounted police force. All are equipped with electric lights and other modern conveniences.

The mounted police is said to be the best force of its kind in the world, and numbers over one thousand men. They patrol the whole Northwest, including the provinces of Assiniboia, Saskatchewan, Athabasca and Alberta, keeping in order the Indian population as well as the rest of the inhabitants who might be inclined to stray from the right path.

Canada's treatment of the Indian problem has long been acknowledged as wiser, more humane and more successful than ours has been, and, as a result, we see the prairies dotted everywhere with Indian tents, the men being occupied with the business of farming or grazing of cattle. They follow these pursuits contentedly and apparently with good financial results. They are well dressed, seemingly prosperous and have overcome their instinctive desire for the excitement of the hunter's life.

What a sad sight is the great square piles of buffalo bones stacked up at different stations awaiting shipment to the East, where they usefully wind up their existence in the sugar refineries and manufactories of phosphates. The men who gather the bones up on the prairies and haul them to the station get six dollars per ton. As an indication of the extent of the business, the quantity sent forward from Moosejaw Station alone is counted by the hundred carloads.

When it is recollected that the few pounds of bleached bones, forming one skelton and bringing perhaps ten cents at the cars, were once the framework of the noblest animal that ever roamed over the continent, and that had he even been slightly protected by law, by common sense or by humane feelings, he would have furnished us with the luxurious robe and succulent meat for years to come, the sight is indeed a sorrowful one. Soon these ghastly piles of bones will be carried away and nothing left to mark the haunts and history of the buffalo except tradition and the scarred sides of the slopes and valleys where he dug out his "wallow."

The coyote we saw very often after passing Moosejaw; also foxes and badgers, and as for gophers, their name is legion. Wild geese, ducks and snipe we also saw on many fresh water ponds and lakes. To-morrow, the 15th, the close season for the prairie chicken expires, and thousands of guns will be cracking away during the day and to the end of the season. We start out at four in the morning and expect to have a chance at a flock of wild geese that settle towards sundown in some wheat stubble a half mile from here. We also intend trying our guns on the plump and gamey prairie hen.

This afternoon we were out snipe shooting for a few hours, and on our tramp passed quite a number of Indian tents and villages, but neither the Indians nor their motley variety of dogs paid any attention to us, excepting one old buck with a red blanket thrown over his shoulders. This fellow followed us silently around, watching us intently, and although saying nothing seemed to be piling up a lot of thinking.

A party of ladies and gentlemen are expected here to-morrow in their private car on a shooting trip to the coast. They eat and sleep in the car, and have been, so far, very successful in shooting and fishing. We passed them twenty miles away this forenoon. They expect to start from here on a side hunt for antelope and bears.

AN OLD "TOTE" ROAD: THE AUTHOR WITH HIS RIFLE IN THE DISTANCE.

I am writing this letter sitting down on the broad prairie beside a palace car (where we are luxuriously housed and fed), waiting until the beds are made up and breakfast is prepared. It is something certainly novel as well as very pleasant to sit down in this latitude to a dinner of wild roast goose, teal duck, prairie chicken, fresh peaches, sweet potatoes, ice cream, etc., with plenty of drinkables besides, and served by competent waiters. For all this luxury we are indebted to the Worcester (Mass.) Excursion Company, who are on their twenty-second annual shooting tour, and who have invited us to join them for the season. Seven gentlemen of the party started, with nineteen horses, tents, provisions, etc., for a hunt after antelopes and grizzly bears, their destination being some thirty miles from Maple Creek. They expect to be gone a week, and of course each man will not be satisfied until he bags his antelope or has had a wrestle with a bear; in the meantime, we that are left are content to worry the prairie chicken and mallard duck with our dogs and guns.

One through train from the Pacific and one from the Atlantic stop here for a few minutes each day, and on their arrival the platform is crowded with Indians dressed up in their best "bib and tucker," which means plenty of feathers, paint and tomahawk. With a special eye to business and the white man's pocket book they come provided with their peculiar wares, such as buffalo horns nicely mounted as hat racks, trinkets of various kinds, pipes, etc. For some reason or other the Indian has a superstition against being photographed. Now almost every train has its kodak fiend, and no sooner does he catch a glimpse of "Poor Lo" than out comes his box and the fun begins. On Saturday one of these enthusiastic fiends tried to get a snap shot at an old "buck" but didn't meet with much success. The moment the old fellow saw the photographer getting ready to point his box he rushed at him with an uplifted stick, jammed him against the car, took possession of his kodak and doubtless would have wiped up the floor with the picturetaker had the mounted police not interfered and ordered him back into the train. Yet the fiend wasn't satisfied. He went into the car and thrust the camera out of one of the windows. Instantly the alarm was given, and every squaw and brave, to the number of thirty or more, dived under the station platform, leaving the discomfited artist to the jeers and hooting of the crowd. One of the ladies of our hunting car, not knowing of this trait in the Indian's character, saw a bunch of squaws lounging around. She got out her kodak and commenced to fix it for a snap shot, when one of the squaws, in her native tongue, threatened her with violence if she turned "that eye" on them. The lady didn't understand the pantomime, and proceeded to take the picture. The squaw very angrily pulled a big stone out from under her blanket and threw it with all her force, hitting her on the wrist, inflicting a painful blow. There will be no further use for the kodak on this car for awhile. The telegraph operator here says the Indian is equally afraid of the "ticker," and it is hard work to get them near it.

On the night of the great prize fight between "Mr." Sullivan and "Mr." Corbett the cowboys, ranchers, railway men, and in fact all the inhabitants of this frontier settlement, were in and around the station. The newspapers of Montana, the Dakotas and Nebraska having formed a syndicate to have the news wired to them in detail, it was sent over the Canadian Pacific wires. The operator sat in his office, and in a conversational tone read the account of the fight as it passed over the wires, when it would be communicated to the outside crowd. Toward the last, when the "big fellow," "Mr." Sullivan, was getting the worst of it, the excitement of the listeners was so great they couldn't keep still. Even the stolid Indian got enthused and grunted his satisfaction, and when the last sentence was ticked out, then pandemonium was let loose. The only hotel in the town was besieged with thirsty customers, and all night long the yelpings of the coyote were blended with the yells of excited humanity.

The Bishop of Q'Appell, who is a baronet of England as well as Bishop, preached a sermon in the little chapel here yesterday that was remarkable for its profundity as well as its eloquence. He is the leader in a movement among the Northwest churchmen which is intended to give new life to the Church of England by trying to arouse it from its apparent lethargy and by claiming for it the undivided support of the people on the ground of its traditions, history and venerable age. In his discourse he easily disposes of the dissenting churches and then in a learned argument he paid his respects to the Roman Catholic Church and proceeded to show that the Church of England was centuries older than the Roman Church. It seemed a great waste of force to preach such a sermon to the little handful of people he had for an audience, but as he leaves this country to spend his last days in England, after preaching here for twenty-six years, he no doubt thought it well to give the people something to think about.

The Canadian Pacific Railway being the most accessible route between Alaska and the East, some very valuable train loads of merchandise pass over its rails. Probably one of the most valuable trains of freight ever hauled in the same number of cars passed through here yesterday. It was a train made up of ten cars of seal skins, booked through to London. Each car was valued at over $200,000—over $2,000,000 in all. The train had a wreck coming down the slopes of the Rocky Mountains. It parted in two ; the back portion ran into the front, smashing things up very generally. What a calamity it would have been—what a rude shock to the American feminine heart had that train and its precious cargo been destroyed by fire ! How many of the "lords of creation" would have been obliged to put their hand a little deeper into their pockets next Christmas if the heart of their better-half should be filled with love for a new seal skin ! But thanks to a providential decree that ordered otherwise, the calamity didn't happen. The train passed in safety and let us hope that its beloved cargo will survive the boisterous gales of the Atlantic and come back to us in the shape of that most beautiful of all the adorning apparel of woman—that warm, glossy, cosy, fascinatingly lovely, but awfully expensive, seal skin sacque.

We reached Crane Lake on September 20th. During our ride in the Hunting car Yellowstone we had matured our plans for a big day's sport, and we got it. I saw more sport in that one day—the 21st—than I ever saw before in a month. To briefly sketch the exciting incidents of the day would, perhaps, prove interesting, as all mankind, particularly the Anglo saxon part of it, has an instinctive interest, more or less keen, in everything that relates to hunting.

AN OLD "TOTE" ROAD; SIGNS OF COMING WINTER.

There were four of us. We got up long before break of day as silently as we could, so as not to disturb the ladies of the party (for, mind you, there are five ladies journeying across the continent and back in the "Yellowstone"). We got away about "five o'clock in the morning," just as the geese were commencing to fly from the lake to the neighboring wheat fields. We were posted along a low ridge, with strict orders to lie down quiet and snug in some thorn bushes (to lie "quiet and snug" in a thorn bush requires practice). When a flock came near we were to jump up, single out a goose and give him some No. 1 shot.

The day was breaking in the East and shedding its faint gray light over the prairie. The dainty colors of the wild flowers, their pale yellows, their pinks and their purples were just becoming discernible in Nature's prairie panorama which was soon to spread itself and rapture us with its beauty.

And now comes the cry of the wild goose: "Honk! Honk! Honk!" Looking up we see a long line of them approaching high overhead. Crack! go the guns and away go the geese leaving none of their company behind. Down we dodge again and another flock comes in sight. As before, another go of the guns and another go of the geese; and thus flock after flock fly over us in their peculiar wedge-shape order, but all too high. However, we venture another crack at them. This time one is seen to drop down a little, recover himself, get back into the flock, drop again a few yards, and then, to our surprise, tumble heels over head, striking the earth a quarter of a mile away. A grain of buckshot did the work.

The morning flight is over and only one goose is bagged. Now we munch a few apples and take the setter dogs and start for the gamey prairie chicken, which out here is really the pin-tailed grouse that goes before civilization, while the regular prairie hen follows civilization. The first bird that is flushed is taken by the youngest shot, my son James—boy of 15 years—and beautifully stopped. The second bird is similarly treated by the same gunner. The birds now are popping up all around, and we all get our share.

We go back to the car, have breakfast, and off we tramp to Crane Lake, about four miles away. Reaching the water, we find it literally covered in places with ducks, snipe, geese, yellow legs, pelicans, curlew and plover. A few shots started the whole aggregation in motion—mallards, plover and Wilson snip begin to tumble until we are loaded with all we can carry. A gunner away off across the prairie is heard to fire two barrels, then to shout, jump, run, and throw his hands up. No one seemed to know what was disturbing him, but in a moment we see two dogs coming at a furious rate. No; one is a coyote, the other is a dog in full chase. Four guns are discharged with No. 5 shot at the slinking coyote, but he gets out of danger in a few minutes. Then a monster bird comes flapping leisurely around the shore. It is a pelican, and, as if to tease us and waste our shells, he flaps serenely by in front of each gunner several times, each time getting the contents of shells from No. 5 down to buckshot. He is hit from every angle, some twenty-five shells in all having been fired at him. We could hear the shot strike and then drop into the water, and yet Mr. Pelican is still "winking the other eye" and will continue to wink it at anything less than a rifle.

With our game belts loaded to their fullest capacity (mine must have weighed forty pounds, although it felt like a ton), we started back, killing more prairie chickens on the road, and arriving in time for dinner (five o'clock), having been out just twelve hours. What exhilaration was crowded into those twelve hours! One who has never been out in this rarified highly electric atmosphere cannot understand or appreciate the glories of such a hunt on such a day—the sun comfortably warm, with a cool wind waving the rich prairie grass and rippling the water so that it shone from the distance like burnished silver. Along the edges of the sloughs which empty into the lake the green willows, stirred with the wind, were waving their graceful limbs, while the bright prairie flowers and the sage brush did their part toward making a picture hard to match and not easy to be forgotten.

After dinner we had singing, whistling (by as good a whistler as ever "cocked a lip") and piano playing (two of the ladies being good musicians). When our concert was over and we were about retiring, a knock was heard at the car door, and the members of the only family residing within miles of the station were announced as callers. So again the strains of one of Beethoven's immortal sonatas and a nocturne of Chopin's were invoked to entertain the visitors, who were two ladies and a gentleman, the latter superintending a ranch of 10,000 acres. The latest fashions, the price of wheat (54 cents a bushel) the climate, the habits of the wild fowl around the lake, were discussed. After a pleasant two hours' entertainment the visitors were shown to the car door, saying it was the pleasantest night they had ever spent in their lives, and so ended our day's hunt and pleasure at Crane Lake, Assiniboia Territory.

For months there was no rain in the regions gunned over by our party and we pursued our sport without alloy or hindrance. When we were on the Frazer River, in Vancouver, six of our party who had started away on a hunt after caribon and bears, returned to the car on

Sunday, after a trip of seven days, during which time they rode 130 miles over an almost impenetrable country, and among the mountains some 4500 feet above tide level. For eight miles of that distance the road was so rough that horses could not be taken through, and the camp stuff had to be dragged and pitched over fallen timber, around rocks, under rocks and over rocks. One of the party claims this to be his twenty-second annual hunting trip, and he vows he never saw anything to equal it for roughness and difficulties. They bristled with every step. One caribou and three deer were shot, and as they couldn't drag their game out of the country after killing it, they gave up the hunt as a bad job and returned to the car, having taken three days to go up the mountains and two to return.

Two of the hunters, Messrs. W. E. Harmon and J. G. Brewer, of Boston, had come out determined to get some big game, even if they had to go alone after it. They hired an Indian guide and a cook, got pack horses and provisions and again started out into the mountains where they proposed hunting big horn sheep up above the snow line. They made their way through from Canadian territory into the United States, arriving at Spokane, Washington a distance of 245 miles, camping up in the snow for several days, climbing around snow peaks in moccasins, but always trying to keep face to the wind. They finally succeeded in killing four mountain sheep and three deer, but the hardships and exposure they endured, as evidenced by their torn flesh and clothing, will keep them from trying it again for some time at least. As years glide by and civilization approaches nearer and nearer to the great mountain ranges, the big horns and wild goats of the snow-covered peaks are pushed farther and farther back, so that it will not be long before these nimble-footed and beautiful creatures will follow the fate of the buffalo.

At Sicamous, a town of about one hundred people, on the main line of the C. P. R. in British Columbia, lives Colonel Forester, who was in China when the great rebellion broke out in which General Gordon won his fame. Colonel Forester was requested by the foreign merchants in China to organize and drill what forces could be hastily gathered up, and to take charge of the defense, which he did so successfully that he was offered supreme command of the forces operating against the rebels. He declined, however, in favor of General Gordon. He has a large number of decorations, presents and letters testifying to his bravery and executive ability, and is quietly and modestly living out the remnant of his days in this lonely hamlet.

The scenery along the Frazer River is of the wildest, most interesting and most startling character. Fabulous amounts of money were spent in the construction of this part of the Canadian Pacific Railway. For a great distance it is a succession of tunnels, trestles, bridges and deep rock cuttings, the line clinging to the bald sides of the mountains and overlooking the Frazer River that rushes along seething and foaming, and in some places a thousand feet below. On the opposite side is the old government road, which was made necessary years ago by reason of the gold excitement on this river, and also to facilitate the valuable salmon fishing. The road is now rapidly going to ruin. We passed thousands of frames of fishing tents left standing by their Indian owners. Wherever the river narrowed to a gorge, there they could be seen in the most inaccessible positions and fixed on the rocks like so many barnacles. How the Indians managed to get there and stay there is hard to imagine.

ALLEGASH RIVER, HEADWATERS OF RIVER ST. JOHN, CANADA.

The town of Vancouver is experiencing a real estate fever of a very acute and inflammatory character. This is all owing to its being the terminus of the Canadian Pacific and also of the magnificent line of steamers running to China and Japan. The town has a population of about 15,000, is situated on a fine bay, with a rich mineral, lumber and agricultural country tributary to it. The grit and enterprise displayed there is such that even Philadelphia might copy with advantage. The Northern Pacific Railroad wants to have an entrance there in order to reap a share in the rich Oriental trade pouring through the town from the great steamers plying to Japan. What did this little town of 15,000 people do to encourage the designs of the railway people? They put the question to popular vote, and the result was that they decided to give the railroad $300,000 as a bonus to enter the town.

Think of it, you Philadelphia Councilmen ; you, who voted so often and worked so hard to keep the Baltimore and Ohio out of the city ; you who kept the Philadelphia and Reading bowing and scraping before your committees for years ; you who kept the Belt Line so long out in the cold, and you who fought so long and fiercely against elevated railroads in our "Traction" ridden city. Ah, there are some profitable lessons that may be learned by getting away from home, and probably there is none that needs a lesson of that sort more than the average Philadelphia Councilman. Let us hope and trust, however, that the Quaker city has got through with her nap and that her eyes are open wide enough to see that when railroads knock at her doors for admission they should be welcomed not repelled.

We arrived at Morley, Alberta, September 25th. The town consists of one store, three dwellings and the railroad station, having a total population of about twenty. It is of importance by reason of its being the distributing point for the reservation of the tribe of Stoney Indians. Large herds of cattle are pastured there by the Canadian Government to provide a weekly supply of meat during the year for the Indians, and the annual payment of five dollars per head is made and blankets distributed in accordance with the treaty stipulations.

The Indians are settled along the valley of the Bow River, some in tepees, but most of them in substantial and well-built log houses, each family having a small cultivated patch of ground on which they raise potatoes, cabbage and other vegetables, while their ponies are hobbled near by and their cattle range the prairie. They seem to spend a happy contented life altogether different from the non-treaty Indians, whose bad traits I observed so markedly in Maple Creek, and whose good qualities were not to be discovered with the naked eye. I talked with a number of those who spoke English, and spoke it quite as well as the majority of white men. They had traveled some, could read and write, treated their wives and families with consideration, and, moreover, had accumulated a little wealth outside of the Government allowance.

One Indian told me that he had not seen his father since he was a boy, until this summer, when his father wrote him a letter asking him to visit him at a point a long distance still further north. He took a team of horses and drove there, the round trip occupying two weeks of traveling. He spent one week with his parents, and spoke of them very affectionately and dutifully.

The Stoney tribe speak the "Cree" language and belong to that race of brave fighters. A Mr. McDougal, who resides near Morley, has translated the Bible and the new Testament (as well as a book of hymns) into the Cree characters (which are said to be very simple and easily learned), and he preaches to them and instructs them in their own tongue. He is a wealthy rancher, one of the oldest residents and has seen the prairies when they teemed with roaming herds of buffalo, elk, antelope and deer   His house contains more stuffed specimens of " animated nature " than any other in this territory.

Some years since an enthusiastic young woman came out here as a missionary from Massachusetts. She was very successful in her work, and among her converts was a "noble Indian," whom she induced to go to college, where he studied faithfully and well, and on graduating was ordained to the ministry. He went back to Morley, made love to the young missionary, was accepted and married her. They are happy, and, while the wife's family is said to have ostracised her, she seems to be satisfied.

Thirteen of our party, including four ladies, started on a chicken hunt to a point some twelve miles from this place. As the Indians indulge in shooting chickens from the saddles of their ponies, and thus depleting their numbers, it was necessary to take teams and drive this distance before we found the birds which even then were in only limited numbers and as wild as hares. When we arrived on the shooting ground it was nearly noon, and as the birds had finished their morning feeding and were found on the edge of the brush fringing a little stream, we had hard work getting more than a glimpse of them before they would be out of sight. Taking long flights made it slow shooting. However we made a fairly good bag, and, as it is always the practice of this party of sportsmen and sportswomen to shoot only what they can use to advantage, we gave up the sport and the hard work in good season and enjoyed a glorious ride back, watching the forms and ever-changing shadows of the Rocky Mountains, which, though eighteen miles distant, seemed close enough to be reached in a half-hour's walk.

We were told that at Bow River all we had to do was to throw in our fish lines, and with any sort of a fly we could catch all the speckled trout we could handle, and that Morley was the point on the Bow which gave the best results; but—how often these "buts" come in to upset trout-fishing calculation, and this particular "but" did it effectually—a roadmaster on the Canadian Pacific had been drowned in the treacherous current and the authorities, hoping to bring his body to the surface, exploded dynamite in all the pools up and down the river for five miles. These explosions, though they did not raise the body, certainly did raise the d——l with the fish, killing nearly all of them. And thus, once more our fond hopes and fancy of hauling in the speckled beauties on our seven-ounce rods were scattered to the winds. After a whole day's throwing and coaxing with all sorts of flies, minnows and bait we succeeded in landing only a paltry dozen or so.

Ten persons having lost their lives in the river near here within a few months, the ranchers, cowboys and even the Indians hold it very much in awe. The water is icy cold, from the melting snow and ice rushing down from the Rocky Mountains; the current is swift, full of eddies, rapids and whirlpools; and the stone on the bottom slippery as an eel. Woe betide the man who should lose his footing in fording or get over head in it in any shape; his chances of getting out would be slim indeed.

We arrived in Banff early in the morning and slipped out before breakfast to see the town and spy out the points of attraction which the Canadian Pacific has set such store by. The town is nil—nein—nix. A few log huts, a small brick church, a dozen or more frame shanty stores, and stumps and fallen trees galore.

But the attractions are there, and they are attractions, too, with no nonsense about them. " Whatever the company has advertised to perform, that it will perform, or your money refunded," would apply very well. The luxurious C. P. R. R. Hotel, about two miles from the station, newly built, superbly furnished and lighted, spacious, comfortable and well kept, is a "number one" drawing card. A sanitarium, a few pretty, small hotels, glorious drives among glorious mountains capped with everlasting snow, a park, twenty-six miles long by ten miles wide, embracing parts of the Bow, Spray and Cascade Rivers; the Hot Sulphur Springs, the Warm Sulphur Springs, bridle paths and walks up the various peaks and the unrivaled landscape all aglow with the brilliant tints of its autumn foliage, make a combination of attractions that has already proved strong enough to draw tourists from all parts of this Continent and a great many from Europe as well—a fact that the register at the big hotel fully attests.

My choice in this list of attractions was to take a warm sulphur bath and then scale a mountain. Now isn't it unique to take a bath in an enclosure open at the top, where the white caps of the mountains are seen all around you and the rain pouring in? And yet we are swimming in a pool of sulphur water at the natural temperature of ninety degrees, and with plenty of room for diving, fancy swimming and frolics generally.

The mountain climb was equally worthy of remembrance. I wasn't at all ambitious of "going" for one of the 6000 foot giants. I selected a modest 1200 foot fellow called Tunnel Mountain, and in face of fierce winds and gusts of rain (which on the higher peaks fell in the form of snow) I scaled it in about an hour and a half. The view from the top was as enchanting and ravishing as mortal eye ever rested on. Neither poet nor painter could even faintly describe or picture it. Why should I then, who have not the gift of either, attempt to do what cannot be done? Suffice it to say, it is imprinted on my memory and likely to stay there.

ONE OF OUR CAMPS.

Coming down, like numerous other would-be smart ones, I thought it an easy matter to leave the carefully graded path and by traveling straight down save time and distance. Very soon my feet slipped from under me; down on my back I slid, grasping at shrubs, stones and plants in my rapid descent, which kept up until its unpleasant speed was stopped by running into a tree. With scratched hands, torn pants, a bruised back and a little more wisdom, I concluded to keep to the path for the remainder of the distance.

Did it ever strike you how many difficulties there are to be encountered, the distances to be covered and the obstacles to be surmounted in the search after speckled trout? It struck us, but not until after we had tried it. We had so many promises of good trout fishing on this trip, with so many disappointments, that when we reached Banff and found that, although there was any quantity of trout there, it was close season in the park, and we couldn't fish we were about giving up all idea of ever seeing one. Just then we stumbled over a fellow who told us of a wonderful little lake, recently discovered and only fished in for the first time two months ago, at Castle Mountain, seventeen miles from Banff.

On the promise that it was full of trout and notwithstanding the warning that he doubted whether we could rough it enough to get there, we determined to go and find out whether he was a fish romancer or not. Our car was pulled there in the early morning. A guide had come with us from Banff, who filled us with bouncing predictions of the luck we were going to have but kept very dark about the difficulties and dangers of the trip. Seven of us started with him, unconscious of what was before us. He had led us along a small creek to a frail crossing on a slippery fallen tree, over which one man promptly tumbled and had to start back for dry clothes.

We then came to the Bow River, which here is a raging torrent, deep and treacherous. Stretched across diagonally was a very long boom, made by strapping a string of two logs together and held to the shore by stout wire cables. It is the only crossing this side of Banff, seventeen miles away. On account of the fierce rush of waters this string of logs was swaying up and down, with the boiling water surging over them here and there, the inner log half covered with slimy, rotten bark, that peeled and slipped off under foot.

The guide had on shoes with sharp-pointed spikes, which enabled him to skip across the logs with the ease and grace of a dancing master; we had on rubber boots, slippery as glass. There were two logs reaching to the boom and over these the guide, seeing we were not in his "skipping" condition advised us to creep on our hands and knees.

Four of us started across with our feet placed crosswise of the logs. On getting about a third of the way over the guide halloed at the top of his voice: "Look out you don't slip over; if you do, hang on to the logs like grim death or you're a goner! No man can swim in this water; he'd be sucked under and into Davy Jones' locker 'fore he could say Jack Robinson!"

This cheerful bit of information had the effect of making us doubly cautious. By dint of balancing and poising, and feeling with our feet for the least slimy places we at last got safely over. We then had time to realize what idiotic fools we had been to risk our lives on such a crossing, and, for what?—a few trout.

We motioned to the three men we left on the other side not to attempt the passage. They signalled "all right," and we started ahead. Afterwards one of the three made up his mind to try it. He labored along very cautiously until near the middle, then over he went into the deep and icy stream. Fortunately for him, he fell on the inside. He was a strong, athletic young man, and managed to throw an arm around the inside log before his body could be sucked under, and by an almost super-human effort pulled himself on to the boom again. Having got back safely he went to the car for a change of clothes. To-day he is full of thanks to Providence for his narrow escape, and well he may be, for his chance of life in that cauldron of ice water was—well, one in a hundred.

CASTING FOR TROUT IN A FAMOUS POOL.

Shortly after leaving the river we struck a good trail up a mountain side. It ended at an almost impenetrable jungle of fire-swept timber, over, under and around which we panted, perspired and labored for an hour; then suddenly, as if by magic, there flashed upon our sight the loveliest little gem of a lake imaginable, circled around by great mountains, with snow reaching nearly down to the water. We at once jointed our rods, and tried "first and last" live grasshoppers, of which we had plenty. Hardly had I struck my line into the water when a speckled beauty took the hook, and then another and another, and for a couple of hours it was nothing but a swish of the line and a battle with the trout.

Soon we had as many as we could carry. Meanwhile, the other three who were left, had, with the assistance of the guide, who had returned to help them, resurrected an old scow and crossed. About two o'clock they appeared with a welcome lunch. The car log book of game credits the party with a catch of some three hundred and fifty speckled trout, certainly enough to last us a few days, as we have them carefully packed away in the refrigerator.

Next morning our car was coupled to the Pacific express and hauled to that wonderful spot, the great "Selkirk Glacier." An excursion was promptly made to the glacier, which is said to be seven miles long, two miles broad and 2000 feet thick, of solid ice. A fine object lesson is here obtained of the resistless power of the ice in crushing, powdering and moving enormous masses of rocks. Avalanches, landslides and terrific storms are of such frequent occurrence during the winter and spring that the occupants of the railroad hotel and station are in daily terror of their lives.

Early this morning a couple of our sportsmen, armed with rifles, started away from the car hoping to get a sight of a bear. Six of them—two grizzlies and one black bear, each with a cub—were reported to be feeding on berries less than a quarter of a mile away from the station. In a very few minutes three shots were heard, then five in rapid succession, then one shot, and we divined that a bear had surely fallen. Excitement ran high and all were on tip-toe of expectation, until two hunters returned—without the bear.

It took some time for the truth to gleam through the glamour surrounding that early morning encounter with bruin, and here it is. A railway employee had located the bears and at daylight crept down among the berry bushes where they were expected to feed, and patiently waited with the determination of bringing one down. The track here makes a sharply defined horse shoe curve, and on one arm of this curve is a snow shed a mile long. One of our hunters had climbed on top of this shed and walked along for half its length when he saw a bear come out in an open patch seven hundred yards away. Now, he couldn't get off the shed without going to the end of it and by doing this he feared he might lose sight of the bear. So to lose no time he commenced firing.

The other hunter saw with his glass a man down in the berry patch and thought hunter number one was shooting at him. The man in the berry patch seemed to think so too, and after his ears had listened to the close whistle of seven or eight bullets he emerged from the bushes and walking up to hunter number one opened up on him a battery of Western words that fairly smoked with brimstone. I'll omit them here, only saying that they conveyed the idea that the bullets had nearly hit him.   "Besides," he said, "how the devil do you expect to shoot bears from the top of a snow shed three quarters of a mile away?"

It took lots of oily words to smooth out the berry man's waves of indignation.   After warning hunter number one that if he valued the integrity of his own hide he had better not try that sort of fun again, but keep his bullets in their pouch, where they evidently belonged, he finally agreed to an armistice and a drink of whisky.

Number two had in the meantime followed the bear away down the river but lost the trail and dejectedly returned, adding his opinion to that of the berry bush man: "The idea of a fellow trying to shoot a bear from the top of a snow shed and across a whole county!"

And now we come to Lake Okanagan to try our guns on the wild geese and ducks.

By the way, like the immortal Mrs. O'Brien, who, when she had acquired wealth and position in society insisted upon calling herself Mrs. O'Brion, with the accent on the last syllable, Lake Okanagan is not Okanagan at all, but is pronounced Okanawgan, accent on the third sylla ble.   It is named after a tribe of Indians (a branch of the Chinook race).   It is about eighty miles long and from two to twelve miles in breadth, well filled with silver trout, salmon trout, chub and lake trout.   The growing town of Vernon, with a present population of about four hundred, is five miles from it.   The lake is bordered by a remarkably fine piece of ranching and agricultural country, and on account of its manifold attractions—the depth and coldness of its waters, the beauty of the scenery, the wealth of wild fowl and its wonderful climate—it is destined to become a prominent summer resort for residents of the Pacific coast near Vancouver and Victoria.

The lake and the town of Vernon are reached by a branch of the Canadian Pacific Railroad fifty-one miles long. This branch, though in operation but a short time (it was opened on the twenty-fifth of last June) is said to be already paying handsomely. Previous to the building of the C. P. R. R. main line all merchandise had to be transported on pack horses a distance of two hundred and fifty miles from Fort Hope, on the Frazer River. The item of freight was then a very serious one, as it amounted to eleven cents per pound on sugar, nails, hardware, coffee and all heavy articles, and a proportionately higher rate on more bulky merchandise. It must be from this reason then, that, although the railroad has been opened over three months and the freight charges are very moderate, the merchants have not got used to the changed condition of affairs.

Everything is absurdly high. You are charged twenty-five cents for a shave, fifty cents for a pint bottle of apollinaris or Bass' ale, and corresponding prices for everything else. But the livery stable men are the real Shylocks of the town. A physician was dilating upon the qualities of a very good young mare he had just bought for ten dollars, and assured me he could buy any number of them at that price. I thought, as horse flesh was so cheap, I should be able to enjoy many drives and see the country without injuring my pocket. The thought was hardly a sound one. At my first trial of it, the stable man charged me five dollars for a very sorry looking horse and a dilapidated buggy whose years might have equaled those of the "Deacon's one horse shay." The charge for a pair of similar looking animals and a similar looking wagon I found to be ten dollars. Such modesty is rare.

We have been here a week, and, while there are three livery stables, all doing a rushing trade, we have  never been able to see the proprietor of one of them to know whether the charges exacted from us are warranted or not, as each of them seems to be more interested in shooting

PULLING THE CANOE OVER SHALLOW WATER.

or horse racing than in looking after his business.

This is truly a wonderful belt of country, the most fertile we have yet seen. The presbyterian minister here (lately preaching at Rutledge, Pa.) tells us that the soil in places is fully fifteen feet deep and of the richest black loam. The wheat averages over thirty bushels to the acre and weighs sixty-five to sixty-six pounds to the bushel. They make no rotation in planting. It is wheat and wheat year after year. We saw a field just harvested that produced thirty-two bushels to the acre which had been sown with wheat for twenty-three consecutive years, and another field of forty acres that last year had not been sown, but simply ploughed under, with the previous year's stubble on it, that netted its owner (a half-breed Indian) $700. Fruits, hops and vegetables are equally prolific.

The climate is dry, with hot days, cold nights and few sudden changes. Even now the days are as hot as in July and the nights cold enough for November. The only doctor in the neighborhood says he never saw nor did he ever read of such a healthy district. Children don't get sick. People eat well, sleep well and live long, and the only business on which a doctor can earn his living comes from accidents or from practice incidental to the natural increase in the population.

The Earl of Aberdeen, Governor-General of Canada, has a ranch four miles from here, which is managed by his brother-in-law, the Hon. Major Majoribanks. He also has another ranch of several thousand acres at Mission, a settlement at the other end of Lake Okanagan. His lordship owns almost countless herds of cattle and sheep and droves of horses and pigs. A couple of young men, relatives of the Duke of Argyle, are now here shooting. So, between the noble Earl's adherents and his Grace the Duke's relatives, the little town is full of fuss and feathers. It's "Me Lud" this and his "Grace the Duke" that on every side. The Earl's lower ranch, at Mission, is to be irrigated and rented out in plots of twenty acres or more to fruit farmers, for which it is said to be peculiarly adapted.

Four of us have been having good sport during the past week, shooting prairie chickens, ruffled grouse and wild geese. A little lake four miles away is almost covered during daytime with the geese and ducks. The geese leave the lake every morning and evening to feed on the stubble left standing in the wheat fields, and on their passage to and fro comes the only chance to shoot them. On arriving here the chief hunter now left with our car, Mr. A. B. F. Kinney, of Worcester, Mass., selected favorable locations for sinking pits to shoot from, and we all went to work digging with spades and a railroad crowbar. After the ploughed surface was removed the earth was found to be almost solid black loam, which reached down as far as we went, nearly five feet, and awfully hard digging it was, as our blistered hands gave proof. When the pits were dug a couple of dozen sheet-iron decoy geese were set out; then we covered the edges of the pits with wheat straw, hiding every lump of fresh-turned earth, so that nothing could be seen which would excite the suspicion of the geese. We had scarcely finished our task when we heard their first "honk! honk!" Down into the pits we tumbled like gophers, and crouching together with scarcely breathing room, we saw flock after flock sail over without giving much attention to our painted sham geese. Then another flock came which had more curiosity. To and fro they sailed by us, circling around to find out if things were "on the square," each circle bringing them lower and lower until we were satisfied they were within gunshot. Then up we jumped and blazed away. And the geese —well, nothing seemed to have happened to them, they flew off apparently untouched, but only apparently; we saw one of them lag behind, then drop a little, then rise to the flock, and in a second or two tumble headlong a quarter of a mile away. Another faltered and fell a half a mile away. We found the first with the aid of a dog, hidden in a bunch of grass; the other, for which we searched in vain, was found by a cowboy two days after.

Thus early in the morning and evening we have been in the pits enjoying this most exciting sport, and have bagged enough geese to supply us with all we can use, and an occasional one to give away. At this season of the year they are fat and delicious eating.

Six gentlemen of our party started on Monday of last week on a "big game hunt" into the district of the Gold range of mountains abounding in caribou, grizzly and black bear, Rocky Mountain goats and mountain sheep. They took with them three Indian guides, a white cook and a squaw to cook for the guides. As their camp outfit had to be carried on pack horses sixty-five miles, when they started off they made a very respectable cavalcade. The roads, as well as the hunting ground, are said to be of the roughest description, so whatever game they bring back they will surely earn, particularly when it is said that before leaving they were compelled to take out a license to shoot deer, costing $50 each. As far as we can learn this license or tax is only levied on Americans (Yankees we are called here) while Englishmen, Frenchmen or men of any other nationality are never required to take out a license. If this be really so, it is only another proof of Canada's vexatious and nagging policy towards her big and wealthy neighbor. It also proves how short-sighted they are, as such a policy will never bring reciprocity, which all Canadians sigh for, but retaliation, which they can ill afford, and which is as unseemly among nations as it is among men.

While in the ticket office at Vancouver, British Columbia, we were much amused at a party of three Englishmen belonging to the nobility of England, who were trying to engage a compartment on one of the C. P. R. R.'s first-class cars. They couldn't "you know" travel in a car with ordinary people; but the ticket man assured them there was nothing else for them to do, as there were no compartments, and the company could not arrange one before the train started, no matter how important it might be to them.

They agreed to pay an extra fare if the smoking end of the car could be reserved for them and they authorized the conductor to tell the passengers that they were cholera suspects or small-pox patients or anything he liked in order to keep the "common people" away from them. But all to no purpose. There was but one alternative—take their "medicine" or stay behind.

It was somewhat amusing to hear their criticisms on Uncle Sam's "frightfully vulga' country and beastly traveling don't you know."

The route from Vancouver, in British Columbia, to Seattle, Wash., lies through a rough, heavily timbered district, where the trees measure anywhere from three feet to six feet in diameter. These are of the red cedar variety and are being rapidly sawed down and cut into lumber and shingles.

Why it is I cannot tell, but it certainly *is* nevertheless—I mean that the railway is literally lined with a row of bursted booming towns; each with a bladder-like name, a big hotel, a public hall, maybe, and lots of saloons flaring suggestive signs, such as the "Blazing

Stump Saloon," "New Idea Saloon," "Three of a Kind Saloon," "Let her go Gallagher Saloon," etc., etc.

Convincing evidence of "bustedness" looms up everywhere. Streets deserted, dwellings vacated and closed, and no visible sign of life, except it be the shingle mills and the woodchoppers' shanties that lie on the outskirts and away from the "avenues" and "boulevards" that grace these silent towns.

A CAMP WITH COOK-HOUSE TO THE LEFT AND DINING TABLE TO THE RIGHT.

A dealer in real estate in Seattle told us that the growth of that town had been very much curtailed by heavy investments in those mushroom growths which offer little or no chance of any returns. Seattle and Tacoma are less than forty miles apart, and as both are ambitious, growing towns, there is necessarily great business rivalry and bitter jealousy. Each city claims the largest population, business and wealth; each claims the brightest prospects for the future, and each also delights to decry the boasted advantages of the other. Our candid and unprejudiced opinion is that Seattle is by all odds the most enterprising and promising of the two. Certainly there is much more life there than in Tacoma, and more public spirit.

Tacoma seems to have been nursed and coddled so much by the Northern Pacific that, in a measure, she has lost her independence. On the other hand Seattle has had to scratch and fight for her railroad favors, and fought so well that she has fairly compelled the Northern Pacific to come off its "Tacoma perch" and hustle for its share of the trade. The Great Northern Railway is expected to be opened to Seattle in a few months, and then the difference will be still more marked.

We have been enjoying the luxury of trolling for salmon in Puget Sound, both at Seattle and Tacoma, with fairly good success, as all our party save one (and he was the professional "lone fisherman" of the party) caught one or more salmon. While the sport was very exciting, I confess I was disappointed at the tame fight they make when hooked. There is a good deal more fight and fun in a four pound bass than you can get out of a sixteen pound salmon. But they are beauties; and when you have them safely landed and lying in the bottom of the boat, they are certainly a "joy forever." Our fifteen-year-old sportsman was not to be outdone by the older hands, for he not only hooked and landed his salmon, but he also landed a trout with the trolling line and spoon, a feat which none of us had ever heard of before.

It is needless to say that the catching and canning of the salmon is a very large and profitable industry. The number of people dependent upon his "iridescent highness," the lordly salmon, for a living and the number too, in all civilized portions of the globe, who find economical and delicious nourishment in his red and juicy steaks, would be beyond the ken of man to tell. Yet it is safe to say that no one product of our Western Hemisphere serves to advertise and popularize the country more than the canned salmon. Millions of tins are annually shipped East or exported to Europe and sold at such prices that "canned salmon" is now rightly considered the handiest, the cheapest, and the most nutritious cooked food of the century.

NORTH DAKOTA.

A sportsman's paradise, in truth, is this
Where nothing mars or meddles with his bliss;
Nimrod himself might envy such a spot,
Nor find his game unworthy of his shot.

— *Whitton.*

DOUBTLESS, North Dakota is the "paradise of the sportsman" but I am not so sure it contains nothing to "meddle with his bliss." Indeed I have strong evidence to the contrary which I will spread before the reader a little further on.

We wound up our excursion in a blaze of magnificent sport at Dawson, in this state. The proximity of the place to enormous wheatfields and innumerable sloughs, ponds and lakes causes all kinds of aquatic game birds to congregate here and in the greatest abundance. All the duck tribe, including the red head, the mallard, the widgeon, teal, black, and bald pate; the Canadian gray goose, the beautiful white goose, sandhill cranes, and the plump, solid-meated prairie chicken, all these are here and many others, awaiting the pleasure of the sportsmen. The latter come from all parts of the country—but particularly from St. Paul and Chicago—with their 10-bores and 12-bores, their retrieving spaniels and their Irish setters.

The town hasn't over two hundred inhabitants, but it boasts of a large hotel, which is now reaping its harvest from the pockets of the lots of men who know how to shoot as well as the lots that don't.

The migratory wild fowl are now making their way down from the far North in countless multitudes, feeding on the wheat fields and ponds in the early morning and late evening, and resting in the centre of some lake large enough to keep them from out the reach of the deadly breech-loader during the day.

The flights of geese are something wonderful, and it is more wonderful still that so very few of them are shot. There is no more wary or suspicious bird than the Canada goose. They will not settle anywhere without first carefully looking the ground over. From the height at which they fly and in the rarefied atmosphere of the prairies they can see for miles, and they carefully avoid any moving object, particularly if it be that of the human form.

We had spent several days there before we were able to discover the fields they were feeding on. When we did find the place it was literally sprinkled with their droppings and breast feathers. We selected a suitable spot, dug two luxurious pits, fixed the edges up with wheat stubble as carefully as possible, set our decoys and jumped in to await the coming of the "honkers." We had been in the pits only a few minutes when we saw away off on the prairie what appeared to be a man with a dog. The man seemed demented, jumping and running around, and lying down on his back, then jumping up again and repeating his operations in the most eccentric manner. We held a whispered consultation from pit to pit as to what was best to be done. It was folly to think that the geese would come down from the clouds for the purpose of getting a closer view of his capers. Oh no, we knew they were not such geese as that; so it was decided that I should be the Ambassador Plenipo with full power to coax, drive, persuade or kick the funny intruder off the prairie. When I reached him I found, not a man, but a stubby, little, barefooted German boy, whose feet were sore from walking over the sharp-pointed wheat stubble. Hence his tears, I thought, for he was crying. But I was mistaken. His grief was not of the sore-footed sort. He was only a "little Bo-Peep" of the prairie variety, and he had lost his sheep and didn't know where to find 'em.

With more ingenuity than veracity, and a very ragged attempt to handle his mother tongue, I told him when and where I had seen them and if he would only hurry away in the direction which I pointed out he would soon overtake their tails.

Watching him until well out of sight and pluming myself on my diplomacy I returned to the pit. I had been there but a short time, when the screaming and "honking" of the first flight was heard, and peeping over the edges of the pit I saw a great moving cloud coming straight for us. But, horrible to relate, there was something else coming, and something that promised to "meddle with our bliss" most effectually. An old black horse with a girl on his back wabbled towards us and getting near enough the girl stopped and yelled at the top of her voice: "Where did ye say ye see my she-e-e-p?" "Oh, for Heaven's sake," I said, "get out of this! Move on! Don't you see you're knocking our sport into smithereens?" But she didn't or couldn't or wouldn't see, until one of our men threatened to put a charge of shot into the old horse unless she hurried him out of the way. The threat seemed to improve her eyesight, for at once she commenced whipping up old "Rosinante" and in a little while both had disappeared in the distance.

And so had the geese. The flock on seeing her had swerved by us a quarter of a mile away, and nothing now could be done but wait for the next and largest flight, which in fifteen minutes we heard coming toward us, fully a couple of miles off. We had just time to ask ourselves whether there was going to be any further meddling with our bliss when the answer showed up for itself. This time it was in the shape of a woman, evidently Bo-peep's mother, accompanied by the rider of the black horse. The girl had ridden home, told her mother we had threatened to shoot her, and now the old lady was here, with the martial fires of her fatherland burning fiercely within her and her blood up to the boiling point. When she got within shouting distance she opened her batteries. She would listen to neither explanation nor defence, and actually charged us with having frightened her sheep away by having a retriever with us, and vowed vengeance. We entreated her, implored her to leave us, to go away, anywhere, so the geese wouldn't see her; that after they had passed she might come back again and we would try to accommodate her with all the vengeance she wanted. But no, there she stood, working her jaws and hurling her brimstone at us, and waving her arms that flew around her head like the sails of a windmill.

The geese passed over and away out of range and sight. Then her arms resumed their equilibrium, and with a few more hot words and a farewell shake of her fist she turned and slowly disappeared over a knoll. And we? Well, we got out of our pits and with spade and shovel silently filled them up again: then, hardly daring to trust ourselves to speak, we got into the wagon and drove to the train, for this was our last hunt for the season of 1892.

BRANT SHOOTING.

This sport, well carried, shall be chronicled.
—*Midsummer-Night's Dream.*

SO let me chronicle the story of a week's sport—
"well carried," I think—on Monomoy Island,
Cape Cod, Mass. A week of atmospheric somer-
saults: a week of rain, snow, hail, sleet, thunder with
vivid lightning, and extreme cold. And yet in spite of
the exposure—twice a day wading a thousand yards to
our shooting boxes, (guided by stakes a hundred yards
apart, while we couldn't see from one to the other through
the fog or sleeting snow) sitting in the box, at times over
our knees in water, the waves dashing over it and slap-
ping down the back of our neck, with the thermometer
hugging close to the freezing point—I say, despite all
this, it was a week that will be fondly fastened in my
memory; a week full of adventure and novelty; any
quantity of ozone; plenty of superbly prepared sea food
for sustenance, and a superbly prepared appetite and
digestion to handle it. It was also a week of total blank
so far as any news of the outside world was concerned.
No letters, no newspapers, no telegrams to side-track our
attention or upset our equanimity. For once, business

and the shop might go to the well, "Hades." Song, story and jest held high carnival. Dull care was banished and his woeful face never permitted to enter the portals of the old club house so long as we held possession. For one week at least he was a stranger, a melancholy tramp, jobless and with no abiding place on the sands of Monomoy Island or the waters thereof.

"Hello! there's branters," said a native of Cape Cod, as we left the little mixed freight and passenger train at Chatham, Mass., on the morning of April 4th. "There be nine on 'em," he said, counting our noses by mental arithmetic; and he was right. There were nine of us, with guns, woolen clothes, rubber clothes, canvas clothes, oil clothes, with leather boots, rubber boots, rubber hats, with crates of onions, boxes of loaded shells, cases of canned goods, mysterious looking "stun jugs" and "sich."

Nine of us from Boston, Worcester, Quincy, Dorchester, Florida and Philadelphia, all drawn together by the Freemasonry of sport, and the shibboleth was "Brant." The day before I left Philadelphia I told a prominent Market Street merchant that I was going shooting for a short time. He asked what I was going to shoot at this time o' year. "Brant," I replied.

"Well," he said, "when I was a boy I used to shoot squirrels with a rifle, and got so that I could shoot them back of the head every time." (How far back he didn't say.)

"Well," I answered, "brant are much harder to shoot than squirrels, for they run faster than rabbits and are much bigger." "Well, I declare," he said, and then relapsed into silence, perfectly satisfied that he knew all about it.

For the information of this Market Street merchant I will say that the brant is smaller than a goose, and at this time of year is on his way Northward, merrily helped along by hundreds of guns belching forth No. 3 to No. 1 shot from all sorts of innocent looking shooting boxes, surrounded with decoys, both artificial and natural.

The brant is here in countless numbers.

It is a bird of beautiful plumage and graceful form; plump and fat, swift of wing and wary and suspicious of anything and everything that bears the slightest semblance of danger. There is also a mystery surrounding it which has bothered the scientists for ages and is still bothering them—namely, the wherabouts of its breeding habitat. The late Professor Spencer Baird worried himself more, perhaps, than any other savant over this undiscovered territory. No living man, it is said, has ever seen the nest or egg of the brant, and no matter how far explorers have forced their way Northward, the brant has always been seen winging on still further North. Therefore the guides out here (some of whom have grown gray in the pursuit of "brantin'") claim that there surely must be an open Polar Sea where the weather is warm enough to hatch out their eggs, and where food is plenty and nutritious, for they come down in the fall of the year fat and sleek as a pullet. The young birds come South strong of wing and as cunning as—well, I might say of them, as Buckingham said of the little Duke of York. "So cunning and so young is wonderful!"

Monomoy Island lies off the mainland in the ocean a few miles from Chatham, Mass. Between the island and the mainland the succulent sea grass waves gracefully to the gentle swell of the tide or the fierce "Northeaster," which, by the way, has been blowing a gale since we arrived.

Sea grass is the natural food of the "brant." The stretch of sheltered water here is large enough to leave the birds plenty of room to move around in swinging columns without coming within range of the sink boxes, and it is only when the tides and winds are favorable that the birds are brought within the line of danger. The "Monomoy Brant-ing Club" (the only one, I believe, on the continent) has a couple of comfort-able houses built on a bluff or sand dune, with artistically con-structed sink boxes placed at the most favorable points and a large stock of wooden decoys. Live brant with clipped wings help to lure their brethren into danger, and with as much apparent satisfaction and enjoy-ment as the setter dog takes in flushing grouse or quail. The club is formed mostly of Eastern gentlemen, all, of course, enthusiasts in sporting, and whose number is limited to twenty, each member being entitled to invite one guest. Four members only are permitted to be here at one time, and, as the shooting lasts five weeks, each set

HOMEWARD BOUND; ON CHESUNCOOK LAKE.

with their guests have one week's fun. At dinner in the little hotel at Chatham we met the party who had preceded us, returning to the "Hub" with seventy-four "brant," bronzed cheeks and ravenous appetites.

Four guides are engaged by the club. They are men who thoroughly know the habits of the birds, understand the tides and currents, and handling of boats, and know how to shoot besides.

One of them has been continuously at the business of "guidin'" for thirty-one years, during all that time only missing two days—one when he had to go to a funeral and the other when he had to go to court. The care of family, the tender offices of friends, the seductions of courtship, the excitement of the play or the circus, none of these has any allurement for these weather-beaten, blue-eyed and kindly men when once the branting season opens. During the rest of the year they earn a comfortable but precarious living by fishing and wrecking. They watch the shifting sands, the gloomy fogs and the blinding snow storms with earnest solicitude, for this is truly a dangerous place for the unwary mariner. Close by the island lies the wreck of the Yacht Alva, which all the wealth of its owner, Mr. Vanderbilt, could not save. Right on the beach lie the keel, the ribs and spars of the good ship Altamah, while her cargo of lumber is strewn on the shore for a long distance, the drifting sand now covering it up as with a winding sheet. This vessel struck the wreck of the Alva, opening a huge rent in her bow, and the lashing surf did the rest. During the winter the fine steamer Cottage City, from Portland, Me., to New York, struck in about fourteen feet of water,

She held fast until thousands of boxes of merchandise were thrown overboard, when, with the aid of a tug and a high tide, she was gotten off, and without rudder or sternpost was towed to New York.

Our friends, the guides, lament the fact that most of the jettisoned cargo floated out to sea, but with the remainder, which was weighty enough to sink, they have been engaged for some weeks grappling in fifteen feet of water, and bringing their find to the surface and shore. Of course, some "odd" lots have been brought up. Among them was a case of 2500 little boxes of split leaden bullets for fish line sinkers and several cases of white, flinty rock, consigned to a Trenton pottery, which the wreckers are much out of heart about, because of their weight and also because no one down here can tell whether they are worth the freight to Trenton or not.

These wreckers, branters and fishermen live a happy life and are as full of content as an egg is of meat. No fluctuations in stocks; no frills of fashion; no telephone reduced rates; no silver craze—in fact nothing under the sun or above it can knock the bottom out of a "branter's" content, give him but the favoring tide and howling gust that bring the brant "in plenty" to his decoys. This it is that warms up his imagination, cheers his heart and fill his pocket with "the coin of the realm."

THE QUAINT CAPE CODDERS.

Ah, what a life were this !

—*Henry VI.*

O N my journey down here, via the Old Colony Railroad, I was much impressed by the evidences on
every hand of the bitter struggle the sturdy Cape
Cod people have to wage at all times to provide the
rude shelter and homely fare which their existence in
these barren stretches of sand dunes, pine forests and
cranberry bogs demands. We can, without any trouble,
read in their faces the story of scanty crops, grown on
poor soil; of continued exposure to wind and weather in
the pursuit of the finny tribe that swim in the numerous
bays and channels as well as in the dangerous regions of
the " Grand Banks " and Block Island, or in the laborious
and patience-trying business of raising cranberries.

The Old Colony Railroad, whose stock is held largely
by the natives of Cape Cod, and who look upon it as the
great railroad of the world, has a time-honored custom of
giving to its stockholders on the Cape a free ticket to
Boston and return, in order that they may attend the
Road's annual meeting in that city. A man owning one
share has this privilege in common with his more wealthy

neighbor. Therefore, if a Cape Codder has five shares you may rest assured they will be entered singly for each member of his family so all of them may make the annual tour to the "Hub." Of course, this was always a great day, requiring the whole equipment of the Road to handle the crowd with safety and dispatch.

Now there are grave stories told that, as the control of the road has changed, this great free excursion is to be done away with, and there are loud murmurings of discontent among the people at the abolition of this old-time custom.

Spicy tales are told of the Cape Codder and his church-mouse poverty, and some of these are sharpened to a poetic point:

> There was a young lady of Truro,
> Who sighed for a 'hogany bureau ;
> But her pa said "Great God !
> All the men in Cape Cod
> Couldn't pay for a 'hogany bureau !"

But, we are here to shoot "brant" not mahogany bureaus, and therefore I will now describe to you a sight I saw yesterday, and one that will linger in my memory as an instance of the wonderful instinct and weather-wisdom of migrating sea fowl.

For days strong Nor'easters have blown fiercely, accompanied by snow, sleet, rain, thunder and lightning, and through these the brant could have made but little headway had they tried to proceed on their journey Northwards. But they didn't try. They knew better than "Old Probs" what the weather was going to be. Yesterday afternoon there was a lull in the storm, a fog set in, and the brant congregated in long columns, flapping their wings and making the most deafening outcries. Our guides said: "The birds are preparing to start. The weather will settle by morning;" but after the fog came a furious gale, with vivid flashes of lightning, loud peals of thunder and down-pouring of rain. This condition of affairs lasted all night, and for once our confidence in the brant's wisdom and judgment was shaken. But lo and behold, this morning the sun arose bright and warm, with a Southwest wind, and up and away the brant were flying Northward. First a series of swooping circles, rising higher and higher in the air, a pause, then off they go by the thousands, in flocks of from three to five hundred carefully marshaled and efficiently led by some old gander, who will allow his followers no rest for the soles of their feet until the Bay of Fundy or Prince Edward's Island is reached.

This afternoon, no doubt, other flocks equally as large will reach here from the South, stopping to rest and to feed before they again resume their journey to their mysterious and unknown nesting place. As the one conversation, the one aim of the "nine on us" is brant, we have become saturated with the theme, and we think brant, dream brant, talk brant and shoot brant. One of the party has been worked upon so much by the excitement that at the card table—for there's a pack down here—he will throw down his hand and wildly exclaim: "I want to shoot a brant!" In bed he will toss wearily from side to side as the others sit and watch him, and he will moan, "I want to shoot a brant." After a while a little tiny snore is heard, then a faint murmur,

"I want to shoot"—another louder snore and a whisper
—"a brant," and then he has reached the land of dreams
banging away at the birds right and left, jumping out of
the sink box to retrieve them from the swift-flowing tide,
wearily carrying them back to the shanty, past ten one
hundred yard stakes—one thousand yards of deep wading
—and then awakening to the crushing truth "'tis but a
dream." But we are all getting our share of the shooting
and even our brant enthusiast will soon have enough to
quiet his excited mind and cool his heated imagination.

A BIG DEER KILLED BY JAMES J. MARTINDALE, SON OF THE AUTHOR.

The cooking at the club house on Monomoy Island
deserves a warm word of tribute. There are two chefs—
Sam Josephs and Frank Rogers—who revel in producing
dishes peculiar to the Cape and Island that are at once
enticing, nourishing and appetizing. Some of their
productions defy my faint power to depict, but I will long

cherish the recollections of their huge bowl of delicious stewed scallops, their quahog stews, quahog pies, quahog fritters, clam chowders, steamed clams, boiled clams, fresh boiled cod, fish balls with the accompaniment of thin slices of raw Bermuda onions, fresh cucumbers, the finest of butter, Java coffee, and water that made my heart thump when I tasted it to think how long, oh, how long it will be before we can hope to see an American city supplied with such sparkling aqua pura! Now, to this magnificent bill of fare, please add ravenous appetites for one and all of us from our open air exercise, and what wonder then that when we turn into our bunks sweet sleep, sleep without bromides, sleep without hop pillows, or without any other soporific spur, at once embraces us, and in spite of the pounding of the surf at our very doors, in spite of the storm and its thunder pounding in the sky above us, we awake not until Alonzo, the guide, says: "Gentlemen, gentlemen, the tide's allowin' in," and everybody gets up.

THE WRECKER.

A brave fellow! He keeps his tides well.

— Timon of Athens.

O X the barren and inhospitable sand dune of four miles long by one-quarter of a mile broad, which formerly was laid down on the old charts as "Malabar" Island, but now, for some reason, I know not what, is called Monomoy Island, a number of professional wreckers ply their risky, exciting and speculative calling. I have always associated, in my mind, wreckers with pirates, thinking that the terms were synonymous. On the contrary, I have found that the wrecker is a man who risks his very existence to save property, both of vessel and cargo, as well as human life; that in the pursuit of his calling he shows rare bravery, great nerve, hardihood of no common character, shrewd wisdom and cunning in disposing of his "flotsam and jetsam" and a knowledge of law relating to maritime affairs that often outwits the keenest Cape Cod barrister.

For a week I have been with four of these rugged sea dogs, all of them seasoned with more than half a century (one of them 70 years of age), and yet when the winds are fierce, the fogs dense, the snows blinding, they are one and all on the *qui vive* for the signals of

distress from some unfortunate coaster, or steamer, or full
rigged ship, as the case may be. To-day I have walked
for miles along the beach, threading my way over and
among a cargo of Southern hard pine lumber of over two
hundred thousand feet, which is piled high and dry on
the sand from the wreck of the Altamaha, a Scotch
vessel, built forty-five years ago. This lumber was sold
a few days since for $2.75 and $2.25 per thousand feet, as
it lies, and men are now at work removing the coverlet
of sand from it, and measuring and marking it. Then
the purchaser will have his hands full in getting it to the
Boston market and to solve the question, not how much
profit he will reap, but, how much will he lose on the
purchase.

Close by the island lies the wreck of Mr. Vanderbilt's
famous yacht, Alva, whose walnut fixtures and trimmings
are even yet coming daily to shore. A contractor is now,
and has been for some time, at work endeavoring to blow
her to pieces and removing the obstruction, the Government having awarded him the contract for about $9000,
(only half the amount the next lowest bidder asked for
doing the same work.) The contractor brought a little
steamer down from Brooklyn, (she is so slow, even under
full steam as I saw her this morning, that I mistook her
for a stationary light ship), and when the tide is at its
lowest ebb he is able to get about half an hour's work on
the wreck each day, as it then lies in fourteen feet of
water. It is thought he will not make a fortune out of
the job.

The owners of the valuable steamer Cottage City,
which came ashore here, the vessel and cargo valued at

$130,000, sent the captain of the life-saving crew, who had given vital assistance to the vessel in getting her off the shoals after she had jettisoned a large portion of her cargo, the munificent sum of $5 for each man of his crew. The captain promptly returned the donation, with the assertion that he himself could easily afford to give his crew that much without seriously hurting his bank account. The owners of a small coaler that was helped off by the same crew promptly sent the men $25 each, which was a distinction with a difference.

Since I arrived here a vessel of 500 tons burden has gone to the bad on the Handkerchief Shoals, which are a few miles from the Island. A fleet of small craft is daily making visits to the wreck, buying and laying in a generous supply of coal for the winter's fires of the residents of Harwich, Dennis and Chatham at varying prices of from $1 per ton to a lump price for what the dory, sloop, cat boat or yacht can hold.

Some time since a vessel showed signals of distress off the island in a moderate storm. The daring wreckers were soon aboard of her, and found the captain, with his wife and children, anxious to be taken off. The vessel had five and a half feet of water in the hold. The captain was half owner. She was well insured, and he did not care what became of her so that she was beached and the crew, himself and family taken off in safety. The wreckers, together with the life-saving service, manned the three pumps, got her under way and into the calm waters of the bay, where she was sold by the underwriters, the wreckers' share of the "treasure trove" being about $40 per man.

Another vessel was abandoned here some years ago which, when the wreck was broken up, was found to have two huge plugs in her side below the water line, showing conclusively that the captain, in order to reap the insurance, had deliberately filled her with water. Then, finding she was sinking too fast, he had driven the plugs home so as to enable the crew to get ashore without danger.

One of the narrators of these "tales of shipwreck" waddles along with one leg bent out from him like a drawn bow. He has had it broken three times, and now, while it will bear his "heft," as he calls it, he can carry but little addition to it without severe physical distress. The first time it was broken was aboard a shipwrecked vessel that he had agreed to stay by—all alone—while a tug towed her into a haven of rest. The wind was blowing a gale. The hawser being drawn so tight as to have little or no "bight," he had become fearful that the strain causing it to fray by rubbing on the sides of the "eye" through which it passed, might part it. While he was examining it the the iron plating of the "eye" snapped and crumbling like an egg shell under the strain, one of the pieces struck him on his leg below the knee, breaking it in three places. He was just able to signal the tug, which was soon along side. A consultation between the injured man and the captain resulted in the latter taking him into Hyannis, Mass., where he was driven to the station in time to take a train for New Bedford, the nearest place, in those days, to obtain efficient surgical aid.

The railroad service at that time was primitive, the time slow, and the track rough as a corduroy road to the crippled wrecker. The journey in the cars alone lasted just eight hours, and during the whole of this excruciating journey he had to hold his knee tightly with his hands. The doctor who set it complimented him on his wonderful exhibition of pluck and grit, kept him in bed eight weeks and sent him home with, as he described it, the "best bad leg" he had ever seen. In these days of anæsthetics and improved railroad facilities such a trip would be of rare occurrence.

Among the Cape's quaint customs I find the old Scottish one known as "bundling" But this, like other of her quaint customs, is slowly yielding to the march of the newspaper, the telegraph, the telephone, and the railroad. I scarcely believed that this custom still existed or, indeed, ever had a foothold on this continent, but I soon found indubitable proof of it. "Bundling," you must know, is a method of courtship based on motives of economy, (the saving of light and fire). It is still practiced in Scotland though gradually dying out there, as increasing prosperity affords broader scope for comfort and less necessity for economy.

A WARY BIRD.

We'll make a solemn wager on your cunnings.
—*Hamlet.*

A MAN, to be successful in brant shooting must be a sportsman of the most enthusiastic type and a fair shot. Moreover, he must possess a good constitution, plenty of patience, and plenty of ability to defy cold, wet and exposure. He must expect many disappointments and a great deal of waiting, for the birds are so wary and so seldom deceived it is rarely he will find them within the range of his heaviest charges of powder and shot. When the chance of a shot is obtained and he downs his bird, the excitement is over quick as a flash and he wonders how it all happened. Let me describe how it is done.

During the early spring the guides have sunk boxes large enough to hold three men. The boxes are placed either out on the bay in shallow water, piling up around them hundreds of wheelbarrowfuls of sand at low tide (covering the same and neatly fastening it down with a sail cloth, so that the rushing tides cannot carry it away) to represent a sand bar; or they are fixed on some jutting point of land in the bay, always using plenty of sand, behind which the gunners are to sit with bowed heads, but with watchful eyes and ears. Out in front of these boxes wooden decoys are fixed on a framework like the letter V, five on each frame, all strung together, so that they turn with the tide and wind, and look natural enough to deceive the oldest gander in the flock.

Then two gunners with the guide wend their way to the boxes when the tide is flowing in, the gunners encased in hip rubber boots, two or three pairs of stockings, a heavy suit (flannel shirts, sweaters, overcoats), and lastly an oilskin suit, if the weather be rough. The gunners get in the boxes, arrange their pipes and shells and bail the water out, while the guide takes from a basket a pair of brant with clipped wings which he deftly harnesses together like a span of horses. The yokes, made with leather thongs, are put on their feet not their necks. They are allowed to swim or wade out quite a distance, being secured by a cord, which is kept on a reel in the sink box.

The particular offices these birds are to perform are (when the brant are flying or swimming anywhere near) to flap their wings and "honk" their wild relatives into danger among the decoys; and it is amazing how intelligent they are in their work; how they get away out of range when the wild birds are being covered by the deadly breech-loader, and how they chatter to themselves with seeming satisfaction when the battery has been unmasked and the fallen birds retrieved. When all is ready the guide gets into the box, and then the trials of endurance, patience and expectancy begin. There is no lack of birds in sight—thousands of them—and their cries at times are deafening, but they keep provokingly far enough off to make you feel as if your head must never again be raised. You soon get cramped, numbed with the cold wind or, maybe rain, or snow or sleet blowing and pelting in your face. But you must not get up.

SHOT BY MOONLIGHT, AND AS WE FOUND HIM NEXT DAY.

Once I sat for over five hours in a box, with rain, snow and sleet driving in my teeth, and occasionally the water from the high tide washing over my back and down my neck, patiently waiting for my reward. It came at last. Up like a flash and within range came five birds, flying down the wind with the speed of a carrier pigeon. We got a shot apiece; three were left behind, while the other two were soon miles away, and our long wait and exposure forgotten. We say: "How did those two birds get away?" "I'll bet they're crippled!" "Watch them!" "They're going down!" "No, they're not!" "Yes, they are!" and so on, but the birds are not ours, that is a sure thing. So you never know when out of the haze, or the clear sky, like a meteor from behind you, or straight on, a bunch of birds may come, deceived by your pair of live "honkers" and your bunch of wooden shams. Or again, a flock may be feeding and unconsciously drifting with the inflowing tide towards your box, occasionally giving a quick, suspicious look, swimming back a little, then onward again, and, of course, to raise the tip of your hat above the brim of the sand bank or to get up to stretch yourself is tantamount to a speedy departure of the "mysterious bird of the North." Therefore it is the man who can stand this sort of work the best who is likely to make the biggest bag. But a great deal depends upon the wind as well, for if the currents of air should be blowing off shore there is not much chance of successful shooting, as the wind constantly drifts them away from the decoys, while they are feeding, and if any should get shot and drop down at long range, they are apt to get out of reach before they can be retrieved.

We were seven days on Monomoy Island, and we had a fierce Nor'easter blowing nearly the whole time, so that what success we had (thirty-six brant,) was solely attributable to lots of patience and perseverance against hard conditions.

But the sport compels you to be out in the open air, to inhale the ozone and the ocean breezes, those twin benefactors that bring to the hunter his proverbial appetite. And, Oh that appetite! You have it and a digestion to wait on it that might tackle a brick pile without getting out of order. There is another thing you have, which is not to be sneezed at—the gratification of knowing that with your trusty gun, your hidden retreats, your enticing

decoys and your unwearied patience you are more than a
match for this the grandest and most wary of all game
birds.

> " Nor on the surges of the boundless air,
> Though borne triumphant, are they safe ; the gun,
> Glanc'd just, and sudden, from the gunner's eye,
> O'ertakes their sounding pinions ; and again,
> Immediate brings them from the towering wing,
> Dead to the ground ; or drives them wide dispersed,
> Wounded and wheeling various, down the wind."

This season the brant arrived in great numbers at
Monomoy as early as February, but finding their natural
food—the eel grass—sealed in ice, they were forced to
wing their way backward, after many attempts to get at
their feeding grounds : the cold weather thus compelling
them to make trips of hundreds of miles to the Southward
before they could obtain their sustenance. But they are
grand "flyers" and a few hundred miles of flight is only
like a morning walk for them, and they don't seem to worry
the least bit about it ; but as soon as the ice melted and the
succulent eel grass was exposed to view, then they arrived
in countless numbers. Some say that between the fifth
and tenth of April more birds were at the Island than ever
were seen before at one time. But the wrecks and wreck-
age there, drew all manner of sail boats to the scene to get
coal and lumber, and thus the birds were continually dis-
turbed in their feeding. They were occasionally fired on
at long range from these sail boats, which harassed and
frightened them, keeping them for hours on the move.
This, together with unfavorable winds and storms, reduced
the total bag for the season to one-hundred and ninety-

seven brant. Such was the result of the work of seven weekly parties, aggregating fifty-seven sportsmen, with an average of twenty-eight to each party, and, as our party bagged thirty-six, we have no reason to complain. Of the one-hundred and ninety-seven killed, one-hundred and three were young birds and ninety-four old birds. This proportion of young birds ought to have made the shooting better, as the young birds (in the language of the president of the club, Mr. W. Hapgood) "are less wary, more social and more easily decoyed, and will carry off less lead than the tough old birds, and then it often happens that the elders are led by unsuspicious youth into places of danger where it would be impossible to coax them when separated, therefore the presence of so many juvenile visitors is always a joy to the heart of the sportsman."

A GLIMPSE AT THE "WHITE."

I'll drop me now the current of my sport
To loll awhile in Fashion's giddy court.
—*Anon.*

HAVING for years made an annual pilgrimage to the
White Sulphur Springs—the "Saratoga of the
South"—it has gradually dawned upon me that
few portions of the globe furnish so much material for
the pen of the novelist and the pencil of the artist. The
scenery is so varied, so romantically beautiful in its
wealth of valleys teeming with fruitful crops, and luxur-
iant foliage that holds half hid in its bosom the modest
cabin of some former slave, while here and there the
roof of the more pretentious home peeks through the
green as if to greet the sun and sniff the bracing air.
All this and in a frame of rugged mountains enchanting
in their wildness, and the picture is complete.

So much for the artist.

The novelist will find it a great gathering place of
the wealth and beauty of the South, with daily and
nightly scenes of revelry, amusement, flirting, and love
making. He may witness the excitement and seduction
of the "green baize table," in a neighborhood rife with
stories of the war, which raged in and about the "White"
during the whole time the direful strife was in progress.
The hotel at one time was used as a hospital for the

Northern troops; at another as a stable and resting place for the Confederates. Being only five miles from the Virginia line, this West Virginia watering place came to be looked upon as neutral territory. Here Presidents from the earliest days of the nineteenth century have been wont to spend their holidays and hold court and dispense official patronage beneath the old oaks that lift their stately heads above the famous lawn. Senators, Representatives, bankers and Governors have discussed measures of National and State policy on the porches of the hotel or under the roofs of its one-hundred cottages.

A Southern colonel who had lost everything during the war—except his love for whisky—came to sojourn at the "White." Now he was never known to have any money, but was mostly always flitting around the bar, waiting for the refrain "come and take suthin', Colonel," which invitation, by the way, he was never known to refuse. In consequence of these eccentricities he was looked upon with suspicion by the manager of the house, who promptly sent him his bill at the end of the week, with the request to pay up. The Colonel put the bill in his pocket and promised to attend to it. A couple of days passed and the manager stirred him up again, this time sending the message that he must either pay the bill or leave. The Colonel asked "Did the manager send you to me with such a message?" glaring at the clerk with a fierce I'll-run-you-through look. The clerk timorously said that he had. "Well," said the Colonel, "tell the manager that I'll leave at once, for that is only faar, and I believe in bein' faar." And he left the hotel. It need hardly be added that he left the hotel bill too.

The Chesapeake and Ohio Railroad, on account, I presume, of its being a rather out-of-the-way route to Chicago, has succeeded in getting the Trunk Line Association to grant it the privilege of selling through tickets to Chicago, with the right to stop off at any station on the line. This gave me a practical opportunity of studying the great value of such a concession. As a number of European tourists have been attracted to this line by reason of the concession, I interviewed several of them and found that all of them had selected the route because they could "break the journey as often as they pleased." So they are jogging along leisurely, stopping at such points as they think will interest them, and thereby getting a much better idea of the varied interests and scenery of the country. All of them had stopped in Philadelphia, some for a few hours, some for a couple of days. They said they were more pleased with Philadelphia than any other city they had seen, and were astonished at its size, its Public Buildings, its Park and its stores. Astonished, because they had "never cared much about Philadelphia, don't you know," as explained by one Englishman, whose complexion showed the blush of forty years acquaintance with Bass' ale.

They were pleased apparently with everything but the condition of the streets; the cobble paving exciting their ridicule, and our roads their commiseration. I said that they must not expect a city which covered more ground than London,—with only one fourth of its population,—which was constantly growing and expanding, which furnished comfortable homes first and streets and street paving after, to be so well paved as a city over two thousand years old, on whose streets Roman Emperors have walked, and whose roads were planned and built by Roman engineers before the time of the Saviour. The Englishman said: "Bless my eyes, I never thought of that; it puts a new light on things here, for, come to think of it, this is a new country, and of course the cities must be new, too."

Oh, but won't these European tourists have wonderful stories to tell on their return! Many and many will be the imitations of Dickens' "American Notes," and many and many will be the foolish criticisms made upon and about us. But our visitors will be profoundly impressed with the extent of the country, with the variety of its climate and scenery, with the restless, irresistible push and nerve of the people, with their material welfare and their prosperity, and they will return with broader views of humanity and the world than they ever dreamt of. In this respect the World's Fair will prove a blessing and a grand advertisement for the nation.

Yea, verily as I have said the novelist might find here plenty of food for his fancy, full of richness flavored with facts and seasoned with all the spice of romance.

The genial Southern gentleman who is superintendent of the hotel, and known far and wide as "The Major," could if he would, unwind many a yarn on the late "unpleasantness." He might, for instance, tell of the time when he, with a troop of Confederate cavalry, was commanding the bridge over the Green Briar River, six miles below here. When from the opposite hills was seen an immense force of the "Boys in Blue" defiling down the long road. When the Major and his troop were discovered, how the "Yanks" put spurs to their horses and how the "Johnnies" started for safer quarters. How they came flying past the Grecian columns of the great hotel with the "Yanks" close after them. How they plunged through "Dry Creek," "up hill and down dale," right over the Allegheny Mountains to Old Sweet Springs, a ride of about twenty miles, before the pursuit and flight was over. But the Major and his command were safe: not a man was lost.

The Major's tales are always full of powder.

Eleven miles from here is Lewisburg, W. Va., the county town of Greenbriar county. To reach it a high mountain has to be overcome, or overgone, on the higher points of which is a stretch of utterly worthless land. The soil, what little there is, is red, stony and incapable of producing anything better than an occasional thistle or a stunted, sickly little pine shrub. An old time stage coach was one hot day toiling slowly and painfully up the long hill, filled with passengers who were making merry over the "pore land," one man venturing the remark "that the man who owned that land must be a d——d fool." Thereupon a long, lanky, West Virginian rose up and confronted the speaker in an angry and defiant manner and asserted "that he owned that land, but he wasn't such a d——d fool as they took him for, as he only owned half on it."

Coming down from a horseback ride on Kate Mountain, one of West Virginia's giant hills, my young son said to me, "Ain't these West Virginia mountaineers quaint people?" I readily answered that they were. I have never seen their quaintness and a few of their other peculiarities equaled.   Old-fashioned fellows, homely, frugal, careless of dress and the proprieties of life generally, eternal chewers of tobacco, iron-clad swearers, and chronically hardup.   The current incidents of time have no claims on their attention unless they relate to the triumph of Democracy or the success of the "season" at the "White."   The latter more particularly, for on it is based their sole hope of seeing some ready cash during the year.   This famous resort furnishes employment to about five hundred "help" in the summer and maybe fifty or more the rest of the year, and thus it becomes the distributing source of a goodly number of thousands of dollars annually.   It would be hard to compute the amount the liverymen, florists, photographers, doctors, musicians and the gentlemen who so seductively preside over the fortunes of the "green table" rake in from the army of guests who patronize this "Saratoga of the South."   Speaking of liverymen one of them, an abominable swearer, promised me he would abandon the habit, which I told him I abhorred.   It seems, however, he forgot his promise.   Here is his letter to me verbatim, which will tell how.

> Pleas find inclosed fifteen dolers to pay youre bill. the reson of delay was, hard times, bad weather, sickness and no money. d——d if I believe there's $500 in circulation in the hole United States.
>   Yours Truly——

I reproached him for having broken his solemn word about swearing.   "Well," he said, "I tried not to, but I couldn't help it; times were so awful pore."   "Why," said he, "I owed a man ten cents who lived eighteen miles off, and he drove in one day and sat around for over an hour when he said he wished I would pay him that ten cents, as he had driven all the way in after it, which would make the round trip thirty-six miles for ten cents." He told this incident to prove the scarcity of money out here.

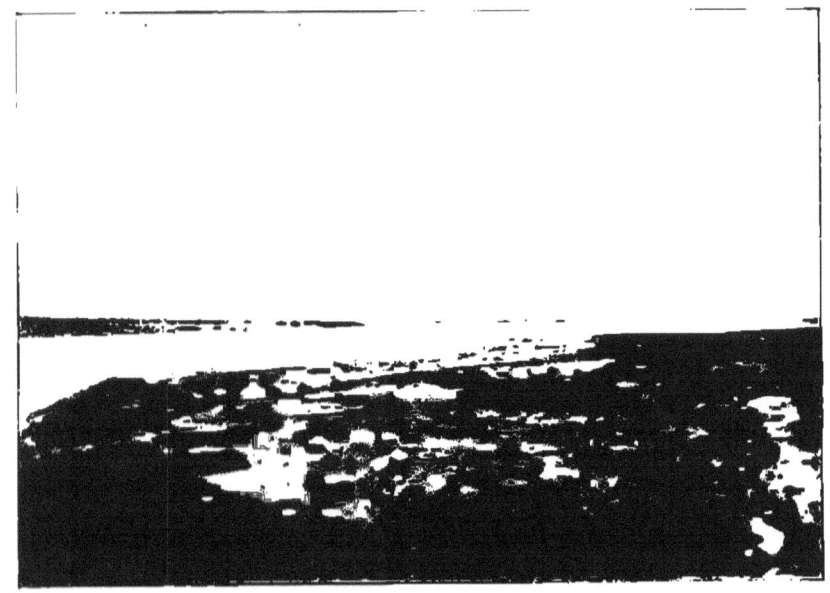

ON THE AMBAZUSKIS RIVER.

Last year a lumberman who had got into financial difficulties allowed three notes which I held against him to go to protest. I was advised to give them to a firm of lawyers in a neighboring town to collect. So I drove over and found that the firm consisted of two brothers, one of whom was that very day in the height of excitement running as a candidate for a public office of a responsible and honorable character. After a chase I finally captured the other brother and gave him the notes for collection. He said he guessed there wasn't much use, but he'd try his best, and putting the notes in his pocket drove off. Last week I happened to meet the maker of the notes, who was joyous over the fact that he was soon going to be able to pay off his creditors, and asked after the three notes. I told him to whom I had given them for collection, but he said he had never heard from them. He advised me to ride to the town and get them, so next day I started over the mountains to see the legal lights. On the road I met my friend the lumberman coming back, and he reported that the lawyers had no recollection of my claim whatever.

On my arrival I found the pundits in a little upstairs room seated at a table covered with envelopes, opened letters, bills of sale, bonds, writs of replevin, leases, promissory notes and "the Lord knows what."

The elder brother was a genial, kindly-looking man, with an old straw hat, a shirt much the worse for wear, and no coat, vest, collar or necktie. He assured me when I told him who I was that he had promptly presented my claim to the lumberman, but he found that if he sued he hadn't any chance, and so had waited. I asked for the return of the notes. Then a hunt was started and such a hunt as only the immortal Dickens could, with justice, have described. Brother number one looked through the letters, papers and portfolios at his side of the table. Brother number two ditto at his side. The day was hot, muggy and oppressive; they got worried, excited and nervous. Brother number two said he guessed he'd go home and look through his clothes, which he did, brother number one in the meantime going through his printed blanks in his search. Brother number two finally returned without the notes and gave it as his opinion that I had never given him any notes. This was awkward on number one, because he had related very minutely just how he had presented the notes to the debtor.

So it was, as an Irishman said, "like bein' in the cinther of a hobble," and with a look of despair, something like the pictures we used to see of the "Knight of the Rueful Countenance," they gave up the hunt and acknowledged they would have to give the debtor a bond to keep him harmless from the notes if they ever turned up, and their only apology for their carelessness was that notes in West Virginia "ain't much account, no how, when they'd got to be sued for," and so they didn't "set much store by them."

At the lumbering town of Ronceverte, W. Va., eleven miles below here, on the Greenbriar river, a great boom and a gigantic saw mill have for years impeded the passage of black bass, trout and other fish up the river, which of olden times was always a noted stream for the bass. The fish used to be of immense size, and, of course, as gamey as black bass can be in cold mountain streams. During the early spring of this year the ice and winter floods caused a break in the big dam which took considerable time in repairing, and lo and behold, the river this summer is full of the fighting beauties eager to take fly, minnow or even bait, hungry—voraciously hungry—and now there is "fishing as is fishing," and the Izaak Waltons are wending their way hither from distant parts to pursue their fascinating sport.

It is intimated that the President of the United States may be induced to come for a few days, as four years ago he plied his rod on the banks of the headwaters of the turbulent James river, about thirty miles from here, at Clifton Forge.   Verily the old Anglo-Saxon love of sport is engrafted in us all to a greater or less extent, else why should it be that the shibboleth of black bass should be more potent in drawing people from a distance than the charm of polite and cultured society, the beneficial properties of the famous waters of the White Sulphur, or even the cuisine of the great hotel and the considerate attention of the Chevalier Bayard of hotel men—"The Major."   But so it is, and I for one would not want to change it.   Let American business men devote more time to outdoor sport, spend more of it in the open air and the knowledge will soon begin to dawn upon them that dollars are not the only good things in this life, and as it can be lived only once, it is better during that "once" to hold on to a share of good health, even though they may drop a few dollars in doing it.

A FIGHT TO THE DEATH.

Both sides fiercely fought.
—*Henry VI.*

WE are a few "city men" up here in the very heart of the wilderness of Pike county, Pa., each man expecting to catch his complement of thirty-five lusty speckled trout, which is all that the rules of the "Beaver Run Club," whose guests we are, will allow any member to kill in any one season (and the fish must be over eight inches in length, to boot, or back they go into the stream).

Japan is said to be the home of the rhododendron, and it is also said that the whole island kingdom is one great bed of those gorgeously dressed flowers. Up here in Pike county is the home of the mountain laurel, which grows and thrives in wanton profusion everywhere about us. It seems to grow equally well on the ridges, in the thick cluster of the woods or down by the edges of the trout pond or its emptying stream; and, behold, it is here in all its glory, and well worth a trip from the heated city just to feast the eye upon its ravishing mass of colors, as the bushes sway to the breeze. The laurel is well backed up by great quantities of wild mountain roses, now in full bloom; acres upon acres of blackberry bushes, clothed with their white blossoms, and also the appetizing sight of the luscious wild strawberries, red ripe and bursting with their delicate acid sweetness, if the term may be used; and why not mention the elderberry and the wild hop vines, both in the height of their rustic loveliness, and the hazel bushes that flourish by the road-side. The man whose sense of beauty remains unstirred by such miracles of Nature's coloring must be something of clod whose life is scarce worth the living.

Maybe, however, if the flowers and waving grasses, and the spear-pointed fields of rye, now nearly ready for the reaper, do not arouse him to a knowledge that nature up here is working her miracles every hour, the singing of the wondrous variety of birds might entrance him, for here the feathered songsters, as well as our noblest game birds, thrive and multiply amazingly. As we arrived at night we heard only the solitary whip-poor-will, and we heard him from every direction. He seemed to be ubiquitous, but when "Phoebus 'gan to rise" next morning (Sunday) then did the bird concert truly begin. For a while it was hard to tell, from their notes, which was which, they all sang so lustily and joyously and well; however, bye and bye I recognized the warble of the gay oriole, then the sweet, loving song of the linnet, then the robin, the flicker, the catbird, the blue jay, the song sparrow, and from across the trout pond the familiar note of "Bob White" which rang out clear and sweet, piercing the early morning air like a piccolo. A Wilson snipe started up from a bit of wet land, and swept away, saying, "Scape, scape, scape," while a pair of sandsnipe swelled the chorus with their piping notes. The red-winged blackbird, the grackle and the mottle-breasted thrush were as busy and gleeful as the rest of the feathered songsters, and I had nearly forgotten to mention the leader of the choir, the bobolink. I heard him singing his rollicking, laughing song with such gusto I thought he would split his marvelous little throat.

But while the birds sang, and the bees worked, and the trout leaped swiftly for the passing fly; while nature seemed glad and laughing at her own handiwork, yet sorrow was in the land. As my friends and I sat around the grateful log fire in the club room, our talk was of the tragic death of young Walter Clark, son of 'Squire Clark (an old and respected magistrate of this county), and of the boy's funeral, which had just been held during the afternoon. The cause of his death was a fight to the finish between the boy and a big and vicious rattlesnake. The snake won and the boy won, for each killed the other. "'Twas a duel to the death," and the story of the fight had to be told by conjecture, for there was no eyewitness. The fight was in the seclusion of the woods, and one of the combatants was dead and the other unconscious when found. Walter Clark was a boy of eleven summers, sturdy and strong of his age, but a fever had left him, as a reminder of its virulence, an impaired mind and imperfect speech. He had one marked trait, a strong antipathy to snakes and hornets, and would gladly fight either when opportunity offered. On Friday last his father, the 'Squire, was working in the field and Walter was helping him, barelegged, with but shirt and pants on. The boy heard the ringing of a cow-bell, and said to his father, "Cow! cow!" His father said, "Yes, I hear the bell," and went on with his work. The boy started down the road in the direction from whence the sound came, and that was the last seen of him until a search was made over three hours after. He was found away from the road, swollen and unconscious, his tongue out and swelled to such a size that his mouth could not be shut. He was bitten on his hands, his arms, his face and on his legs, and some twenty feet away from him was a great rattlesnake with its back broken in three places, its fangs inserted in its own body, forming a loop. A brother of Walter's, also a lad, had found him and carried him on his back for over a mile and a quarter, until his strength gave out and he fell by the wayside. His father ran out, found the two boys and at once started to doctor the wounded one. Repeated doses of whisky and milk brought the boy back to consciousness for a while, when, with fierce look and gesture, he would shout, "Dam'd snake! dam'd snake!" but convulsions set in and he soon died. His body became spotted like the snake's, with streaks up his chest and sides, and spots upon his cheeks and brow.

It is surmised that after breaking the rattler's back with his stick he rushed at it and caught it in his hands, trying to crush its life out, but that it bit him over and over again wherever it pleased, and finally fastened its fangs into its own body, and then the boy fell back in a swoon. A wagon was sent post haste to Stroudsburg for a coffin, but none could be had in that rustic town, and it was necessary to send to Easton for one. And so the savage, plucky boy has now been laid beneath the sod, and the neighbors and visitors to this wild region revel in stories of snakes, of snake bites and snake fights, and the men hereabouts look carefully where they tread, and jump at the rustling of every chipmunk that they hear, and the women—God bless them—they hug the seclusion and safety of the boarding-house or hotel porch and will not wander "afield" for love or money. Who can blame them. There are many more snakes up here just as deadly as the one that killed Walter Clark, and since the date of our mother Eve women have always dreaded snakes and ever will until the end of time when all our fears will be blotted out, masculine as well as feminine.

A LOST MAN AND A WOUNDED MOOSE.

I have lost my way.
—*Antony and Cleopatra.*

IT is the unexpected that always happens in hunting. When you most desire and look for your game, then is the time you don't see it, and when and where you don't look for it, then and there you're apt to run against it.

My guides had told me marvelous tales of the hunting opportunities that flourished around a certain pond or small lake, a couple of days journey from our camping ground. To find out whether these tales were true or not, I thought it worth while to go there, especially as one of the guides had spent the previous winter in a lumber camp near by, and was familiar, or ought to have been, with the country. There was a very large bog, five miles long and about a mile broad, which was a favorite haunt of the caribou, moose and deer, who found in it enough rich food for sustenance without resorting to any other locality.

Very pretty and promising all this, but "there's no rose without a thorn," and this rose of ours had one in the shape of a goose—a goose of a sportsman who was camped on a stream some two miles away from the pond.

The "goose" delighted in firing a rifle that burnt one hundred grains of powder behind a fifty calibre bullet and enjoyed himself hugely in loading up his miniature cannon and banging away at red squirrels, partridges and rabbits. He would leave his camp in the morning, walk to the pond and make the welkin ring for miles around with the noise of his snap shots and sight shots.

The unwritten law of Maine in regard to the shooting rights on ponds or small lakes is that the sportsman who first puts a canoe upon a pond or small lake is safe from intrusion on the part of any other sportsman. Acting upon this hint we determined to paddle up a stream as far as we could, then carry our canoe to the pond and take possession, thus shutting out our noisy friend. So at four o'clock one morning, our strongest guide started, and after carrying his canoe on his back for a distance of two miles, placed it on the pond and returned to camp for breakfast. Then after our morning meal I started with another guide and walked to the pond loaded only with a tin cup, an axe and a rifle. We reached the pond at about half-past seven, got into the canoe, but at the very first dip of our paddle we heard the boom of the 50-100 rifle fired by our "goose" who was busy banging away at the red squirrels on the other side of the pond. This was not a cheerful state of affairs to contemplate. Big game, as a rule, don't like cannonading nor a neighborhood that indulges in it. A few minutes after the noise of the shot and its echoes were sobered into silence, we saw a pair of deer two hundred yards away. My guide suggested that I try a shot at them, saying it would be a good idea, even if I missed the deer, for it would let the goose—the other fellow—know that there was a canoe on the pond, that the pond was mortgaged and he had better skip. The deer, however, were in an awkward place to be shot at with effect. However, I did shoot and missed. They wheeled like a flash and bounded into the woods. The sound of the shot reached the goose with the 50-100 rifle who stepped out into the open, saw us, and started back for his camp.

We now paddled to the other side of the pond and as the sun was coming out warm we left our coats and vests in the canoe, took with us a tin cup and four bouillon capsules and left, feeling sure that the cannonading already indulged in would hinder us seeing any more game that day. We left the canoe exactly at eight o'clock (I know, for I looked at my watch on starting). Not more than five minutes later my foot stumbled in the bog. Recovering my foothold and looking up I saw a sight that startled me almost as much as the ghost of Hamlet's father startled the melancholy Dane. Not a hundred yards away a great bull-moose, with wide-spreading antlers and dilated nostrils stood looking straight at me from between two trees. The place where he was standing was one where a man would least expect to see him, because, by all rules of prudence and usually safe moose conduct, the noise of the late rifle shots should by this time have driven him miles away from this locality. It appears it did not. And what did I do under the circumstances? Well, precisely what any other man would have done. Up went my rifle and without sighting or even an attempt to take careful aim, I blazed away. And the moose? Ah! Like a ghost he came and like a ghost he disappeared. The guide—a French Canadian—said: "Vat you shoot at?" "A bull-moose," I replied, "Didn't you see him?" "No, I no see him!" "Well," I said, "we'll take up his trail and see if he's hit." "You no hit him," he answered disdainfully.

We tramped around trying to find his tracks without much hope of seeing the tell-tale drops of blood, for the bog was soft and the feet of the moose left no mark as he ran, and the red moss that covered the bog prevented the blood—if there was any—from showing on it. We finally worked out of the bog on the ground leading up to a ridge, and making careful search as we walked, found at last, a drop of fresh, hot blood on a leaf; then a little further on a pool of blood that would have filled a bucket. This blood was mixed with the pink tissue of the lungs, showing plainly that the bullet had gone through that organ of his anatomy. I now proposed to spot the trees so that we could find the place again, then go back to camp and give the moose a chance to lie down and bleed to death. My French Canadian, with a whiff of his old clay pipe, gave it as his opinion that the bull was mortally wounded, that we'd find him in a few minutes and advised that we follow him at once. We did so, finding no difficulty whatever, in tracking him, as his trail was almost a continuous stream of blood, excepting when his wound would apparently become clogged with a piece of the pink tissue, and then for a few yards we would lose his trail, but only for a few yards, for soon the gushing blood would spurt its passage through, forming another pool. And thus we followed on, over ridges and through swamps and bogs, hoping soon to catch a sight of our expected prize. Sometimes we would strike a place where the bull had stopped to listen ; and again where he had gone around a windfall, showing he was hard hit if not mortally wounded. How did we reach these conclusions? Simply enough. The hunter, if he be anything of a detective, which he should be, on seeing, as we saw, a plainly drawn half circle of blood, would say, " Here he stopped and turned half round to listen." In

ON A PILE OF SAWDUST.

the second instance, if he had not been hard hit he would have gone over the windfall and not around it. Once we saw where he had leaned against a tree, either to rest or listen, or both, but nowhere was there any evidence that he had lain down. Twice in our pursuit we heard him crashing through the brush ahead of us, but at neither time were we fortunate enough to catch a glimpse of him.

Our brain befuddled with the chase,
We took no note of time or space,

and before we were aware of it the morning hours had gone and we found ourselves on the borders of another lake, miles away from our canoe and from our camp.

It was three o'clock in the afternoon, when we built a little fire, heated some water in our tin cup and boiled a bouillon capsule for each of us which we drank. The next consideration was " what shall we do now?" The guide said we were about four and a half miles from the canoe, and that in following the twists and turns of the wounded bull we had covered a distance of about eighteen miles. His advice was that we start at once for our canoe, but first to "spot" the trees with the axe to enable us to take up the bull's trail again and track him to his death bed. So at half-past three we started back, the guide assuring me that he knew the way perfectly well. Maybe he did, but coming events cast a sort of a shadow over my mind—maybe he didn't. He first led us through an alder swamp, that only needed a Bengal tiger or two to rival an Indian jungle. Lathered with perspiration we finally got through this and faced a high ridge covered with numerous windfalls After scaling this and getting down on the other side of it we found ourselves in a dense cedar swamp, wandering here and there, and perspiring at every pore with the labor of climbing over and under logs, and jumping windfalls. Then came the pleasant conviction: "We are lost!"

It was nearly dark, the weather had turned cold, and no time was to be lost in getting some wood together and starting a fire. Here we were in what might righteously be called a constipated predicament: without coat or vest, or blanket, or tent, with nothing to eat and nothing to drink. Could we have found water our remaining two bouillon capsules would have made us a good supper; but there was no water and consequently no supper. The best and only thing to do now, I did. I pulled off my hip rubber boots, intending to use them for a pillow, dried my few clothes, wet from perspiration, and kept close to the fire to avoid catching cold from the bare ground and freezing air. My purpose was not to sleep, but keep awake. "Tired Nature," however, wouldn't be denied her "sweet restorer," and soon I was in a slumber that lasted till eleven o'clock, when I awoke to find the cold intense. Piling more wood on the fire, I threw myself again on Mother Earth's bosom and slept till two, when the frost settling on my face like sharp needles awoke me. Again I replenished the fire and again slept till five, when I awoke in time to catch Aurora at her morning task of decorating the oriental sky. And, I may safely say, I never watched her with greater satisfaction, for never before was daylight so welcome to me.

Our search now was for water, but we succeeded in finding none. We did find, however, under an upturned cedar root, a thin sheet of ice. This we broke and melted in our tin cup over the fire and then cooked our capsules in it. Such was our breakfast, and I am rather sure the Roman glutton Lucullus never experienced greater satisfaction over one of his ten thousand dollar dinners than we did over that simple meal of bouillon.

After our breakfast we found a lumber road and followed it for about three miles to a great marsh or meadow. Here we obtained our bearings, discovering that we were about five miles from camp which we reached at eleven o'clock that forenoon, thankful and happy to see once more our white tent and the guide we had left behind whose anxious face told plainly of his alarm at our absence. He had been firing shots at frequent intervals during the night, but the distance between us prevented our hearing them. We had been tramping around an ever-widening circle, until night compelled us to stop. My French Canadian guide, who was one of the "I-know-it-all" men, had nothing to say in extenuation but this: "I don't compre' how it all did happen. I did know ze way sure, and then I didn't. I feel much sorry, but ze nex time I go by ze compass not by ze knows how."

ADVENTURES OF A DEER HUNTER IN MAINE.

Escaped with the skin of my teeth.
—*Job XIX. 20.*

OF all the things in this world which are not pic-
turesque the breaking of camp after a long season
spent in the woods of Maine comes close to being at
the top. We had spent many long and exciting days in
the wilds of Maine, and camp was broken at six in the
morning. The camp had been on a high ledge, overlooking a circular sheet of water, known as Moose Pond,
and flanked by bogs on two sides, a cove at one side and
the outlet into it from a small lake above. It was a
dismal day, and the three guides looked glum when we
started to make our way out of the pond through the
cove into the lake beyond. The wind blew directly in
our faces, and the guides seemed to be afraid of everything. First they were afraid they could not get the
canoes around the point, then afraid they would have to
camp on the shore of the cove,—in fact there was nothing
they were not afraid of. Finally, my son and I told them
that if they would only put us on the other side of the
cove we would lighten the canoes by walking the three
miles across the point and through the woods.

Well, we started, and, although it rained buckets of water, I rather enjoyed the experience. We found many fresh tracks of big game, the windfalls were few, and as the path was deeply carpeted with fresh fallen leaves the walk was anything but tedious.

As I emerged from the forest the road led through a piece of burnt land. I heard a cow-bell jingling, and soon spied some cattle feeding off to the right and straight in front of me two big does. But they had scented me, and as they threw their heels up and bounded away I tried a shot at the nearest one, but—ah, there's that "but" again!—I missed, and the deer were, in a twinkling, safely into the timber.

We reached the lake, and then had a long wait for the canoes. On their arrival we found one of them had shipped a good bit of water, and that they all had had a narrow call from capsizing. As the wind was increasing every minute, and it was necessary for us to cross the lake (here about a mile and a half wide), we put the baggage into one canoe, and with our strongest guide to handle the stern paddle and I to use the bow paddle, while my son squatted down in the centre of the canoe, we pushed out into the hissing, boiling water. The wind was blowing a gale straight down the lake, and so strong as to pick the water up from the top of the white caps and blow it around us in the shape of fine spray. Our course lay diagonally across or up the lake in the teeth of the gale, and hardly had we gotten a hundred yards from shore before my son's "souwester" hat was knocked off by the guide's paddle. But that was no place nor time to stop for a hat. The canoe mounted and rode the waves beautifully, and yet at times it seemed as if the wind would blow us over, or actually out of the water, particularly when we reached the centre of the lake and the canoe was turned obliquely down towards the other shore. Then we had to paddle for our very lives, and to watch the waves and see that they didn't break over us. When the light canoe was going down the sloping sides or in the hollow of a big wave we had to use every pound of our reserve strength to shove her along before another mountain of water caught us. It was indeed a ticklish trip, for had we capsized we would have had no show whatever in the icy water, as our heavy hip boots would have prevented any chance of swimming or of a rescue. We fully appreciated the situation. However, we got over without mishap, other than a wetting, a lost hat, and a profuse perspiration from hard paddling. We were safe and for this we devoutedly thanked the Ordainer of all things

We stopped for dinner at a little frame hotel, the "Chesuncook House," which is the last sign or semblance of a hostelry you see before plunging into the great wilderness beyond. Among those who were making the hotel their headquarters were three "sports" who went out in the morning to hunt and returned at night to recuperate. They had killed a nice buck the day before our arrival and had set it up on the shore of the lake for inspection. It was hanging from a trident formed of three poles, and while the rain beat upon it and the wind swayed it to and fro, the hunters watched it with admiring eyes; and well they might, for it was a beauty.

Now two of the aforesaid sports were from Woodbury, N. J. and the other from Boston. The Boston man and one of the Woodbury men were built on the corpulent model, extremely oily, and with a girth that might have rivaled Falstaff's. But they were not sensitive on that point as some oleaginous men I know are: men to whom the slightest reference or even glance in a stomachward direction would be at once a *casus belli*.

Our conversation at dinner turned upon the treatment they had been experiencing from their guides. "Do you know," said the Boston man, "I have had the most unpleasant experience rubbed into me by these guides and I don't care to have the operation repeated."

"What was the nature of the operation?" I ventured to ask.

"Well, you probably have noticed that I have a good deal of butter in my make-up, and I don't care to have it all melted at once, which seemed to be what these guides were after. They told us that the Ambezuskas meadow was a glorious place to hunt in, and so it may be for a lean man; surely no fat man could find any glory in it unless his fat be of a tougher quality than mine. Imagine three hundred pounds of flesh floundering through mud and water, tripping over cedar roots, falling over logs, struggling for a little temporary foothold in order to pull oneself out of the mud and regain an upright position while the guide stands at a safe distance away, beckoning and shouting "come on!" After this part of the programme had been repeated several times, always winding up with "come on," tired Nature gave out and refused to comply with the guide's mandate. Mounting a stump I gathered together what little strength I had left and put it all into a shout, "You be d——d! I'll not 'come on' any more. 'Come on' yourself, that's what I'm paying you for."

His story, by the way, reminds me of another which is short enough and good enough to fit in here. Two would-be deer hunters, one thin and wiry, the other round and oily, had struck a trail, and the thin fellow lifting his eyes saw a big buck bounding directly towards them. "There he comes! lie down!" shouted the thin chap, but seeing no reduction in the obtrusive size of his companion again he shouted, "Lie down! Lie down!"

This time an answer came from the direction of the butter pile.

"D——n it all, I am lying down!"

"The d——l you are! Then stand up and perhaps the buck won't see you!"

We left Chesuncook Lake at half-past one in the afternoon, fixed our loads in the canoes for our up-river trip at a landing stage, near the mouth of the river, and still in the driving, pitiless rain, we started to paddle up the river, intending to reach the "Halfway House" (a resort for lumbermen, freighters and sportsmen, about eleven miles up the river,) before dark. On the trip up the "sport" is expected to leave the canoe and walk around the obstructions in the stream known as the "Pine Stream Falls," "Rocky Rips," and the "Foxhole Rapids," while the guide with the lightened canoe poles it up against the swift current which swirls and eddies around the huge rocks lying in all sorts of ways and angles in the bed of the stream. We walked therefore through a path in the woods around "Pine Stream Falls" and the "Rocky Rips," and above them was a stretch of "dead water," which ended at the foot of "Fox Hole Rapids." Here we left the canoes again, and took to the road, which runs in a pretty straight direction, while the river makes a great bend off to the right, and the road for the distance of, say a mile and a half, cuts off quite a detour in the river. Just as we entered this road I told my son to walk on ahead very carefully until we came to a piece of burnt land, that I recollected as being quite a feeding ground for deer, as he might get a shot. As he was emerging from the woods on to this burnt land I saw him stop, and take his rifle from under his arm (for it was still pouring rain) aim, and fire. I saw a deer bound away and the youth jumping over burnt timber and scrambling through stunted brush. Again I saw him aim and fire, and I saw the deer drop. Now we were in a pickle; night was coming on fast and the canoes were away off to the right. The rain was splashing down in torrents. There was no time to wait, so we at once opened the deer and took out the "inwards," cut a sapling with our knives, ran it through the "hocks" of the deer, slung it on our shoulders and started for the road. This road is called a "tote road" by courtesy, and in winter it is much used for hauling supplies on when there is a good depth of snow.

In summer and fall it is not much used, and there are rocks upon it, roots upon it, and holes in it, that would shame the "Slough of Despond." It was now dusk, and soon—oh, so soon—it became pitch dark, and the rain, how it did pour! We stumbled and slid along "uber stick and stein," and also over roots and "stein," and water and mud, swaying from side to side with our unwieldy load, rifle in one hand and the other steadying the pole on our shoulders, every now and then tramping on the deer's head, which hung and dragged on the ground. So for the mile and a half we trudged and trudged until the canoes were reached.

Here we found the guides angry and alarmed at our prolonged absence, and, as they were soaking wet, we couldn't blame them. We got into the canoes again and paddled as hard as we could until a welcome light shone ahead at the "Halfway House." This house is away up on a clay bank, set far enough back from the river so that the spring and fall floods won't wash it away. Now a steep clayey bank on a night when the water is pouring down is not a nice one for a lot of half-frozen, half-drowned men to clamber up. We slid and slipped here and there, now down and now up, until we were well covered with clay, but we were cheerful withal, and that's a great deal towards contentment. We at last reached the house, had our baggage brought in, and, to our disgust, found everything was wet, overcoats, blankets, underclothes, negatives, etc., etc. A big fire was built in a big stove. We ate supper, hung our wet clothes around the fire, emptied all of our luggage sacks and hung the contents of them upon the chairs and benches as well as upon the wall, and then to bed, where we slept the sweet sleep that comes to all men who labor out in the open air, and who whimper not at storm or cold but try to make the best of everything that fortune is pleased to shower upon them.

At half-past three the next morning we tumbled out of bed, ate a hasty breakfast of bread and butter and bacon and coffee, repacked all our things (which now were dry) in their proper sacks, carried them down and placed them in the canoes and before the goddess of morn had time to get her eyes open we pushed off for our last canoeing trip of the season.

THE HOUSE THE BEAVER LIVES IN.

The pouring rain of the night before had ceased and now the weather had turned so cold that the water froze upon our paddles, and the river was so nearly frozen that there was little or no spring in the canoes. 'Twas a dead push all the way up to the " Northeast Carry." Our leather boots we had not been able to draw on, by reason of their soaking of the night before, and rubber boots had to be substituted, which, in that biting cold, made it uncomfortable paddling. After a run of four miles we were glad to push the canoes ashore, build a fire and warm up. At about nine o'clock we landed at the "Carry," hired a wagon to "tote" our stuff over to Moosehead Lake and then we walked the two miles of good road, which constitutes this famous "Carry."

At the little hotel at the lake end of the "Carry" we had to wait several hours for a steamboat to take us to Greenville, forty miles away, where the train is taken for Bangor. Here I noticed a youth who looked feeble and sick, as if nigh unto death. He was a farmer's boy, whose home was near Hartford, Conn. On the farm he had read and reread stories of hunters; of their happy lives in the woods, and their ignorance of restraint. The reading of Cooper's novels had so fired his imagination he believed that all he had to do to be and live the life of a hunter was to take into the woods with him a rifle and a rubber blanket. This was not a theory with him to dream over, but one to act upon, and in reality that was exactly what he did. He came alone from his farm, went alone into the woods and very soon stalked a deer which he succeeded in killing. Then his youthful breast beat high with rapture as he saw the noble quarry lying at his feet. But hunger must be appeased, and he was hungry, no doubt about that. He dressed the deer, cut a steak, still reeking with animal heat, built a fire, toasted the venison on a stick and greedily ate it. Then spreading his rubber blanket upon the ground and without either blanket to cover him or sleeping bag to crawl into, he laid him down in the frosty air and slept the sleep of youth and tired-out nature. Next morning he awoke with shivering body and chattering teeth and a burning pain in the intestines. Hanging his deer up in a tree as well as he could, he built a fresh fire and tried to warm his body and dispel the chill which at last gave way to a fever and a splitting headache. The morning passed, noon came, and night, and there he lay. On the morning of the second day, prone upon the ground, with the red squirrels busy about him gathering their winter stores, the poor boy lay. Here, sick, far from home, from kindred, from a mother's tender care, from a doctor's aid, he was found by a party of lumbermen, who carried him to their camp and nursed and fed him as well as they could for six days. Then as the winter was fast closing in they sent a man out of the woods with him to the "Carry," and here I saw him. His attendant asked me if I would look after him as far as I went. I told him nothing could give me more pleasure than to do so.

When the steamboat arrived I took him aboard, got a sofa for him to lie upon, and then looked my medicine chest over. Picking out some tablets, which had a very little morphia in them, I gave him one of these every three hours, and made him drink hot milk with some cayenne pepper in it.

We reached Greenville very late at night, leaving at six the next morning and arrived at Bangor about noon, which place we left sometime in the early afternoon. At these places and wherever and whenever I could get the hot milk I made the poor boy drink it. At Portland, I had a doctor examine him who said that the boy was certainly in the early stages of typhoid fever and that he also had intestinal catarrh, caused by the eating of the venison before it had parted with its animal heat. The doctor also said that the tablets I had given him were "right" and that the hot milk was "right." We reached Boston at nine o'clock in the evening, and thinking that the train I was to take was the same which was to carry the boy to his home, I took him to the Providence depot, but found I was mistaken, and that he had to go by the Boston and Albany Railway. My time was short and his too Checking my own baggage I engaged my berth to Philadelphia, and leaving my son with the remainder of the stuff, started for the other depot. It was raining heavily, and at that time of night I could find neither carriage nor street car, and so was compelled partly to support and carry, and partly to drag the sick boy on the way. We reached the train with five minutes to spare. After buying his ticket I helped him into a car, laid him down and then hunted up the conductor—a portly, pompous, beggar-on-horse-back sort of a fellow—and asked him if he wouldn't kindly look after the boy to the end of his division and then ask the following conductor also to see to his comfort. His reply was perhaps what I might have expected. "No, sir! I have no time to look after sick people. I've got my train to attend to, and if the boy gives me any trouble I'll put him off at Worcester and send him to the hospital." A man was standing near him (probably a railway official) who had listened to my story and request and to the conductor's reply. He turned quickly to the man of brass buttons and swinging lantern, and spoke with a frown. The words were few and their purport I did not catch, but, whatever it may have been, the change was magical. The conductor came toward me and in the most polite and cringing manner promised to look after the boy. Then the semaphore over the gate changed from red to white, the bell rang, a shout of "All aboard" and with measured puff the train was on its way.

My own train was to leave at midnight and I hurried back to it through the rain which pelted in torrents and wet me through. However, it took but little time to get undressed and into my berth. A few moments afterwards I felt the train moving out of the station, and then all knowledge and recollection took a back seat. I knew nothing until I awoke next morning in Philadelphia, fully aware then that the hunting season of 1896 was over, that I was back among my friends and loved ones, sound in mind and limb, revived in brain and ready for any amount of work. Verily.

> " Hunting is an exercise
> To make man sturdy, active, wise ;
> To fill his spirits with delight,
> To help his bearing, mend his sight,
> To teach him arts that never slip
> His memory ; canoemanship,
> And search and sharpness and defense,
> And all ill habits chaseth hence."

THE YOUNG HUNTER.

JAMES J. MARTINDALE AT 13 YEARS, WHEN HE KILLED HIS FIRST GAME.

A PARTING SHOT.

PLUTARCH says: "Recreation is the sweet sauce
of labor," a fact of which the American business
man who usually swallows his labor with no sauce
at all, should make a note.

"What so strong
But wanting rest, will also want the might?
The Sun that measures heaven all day long,
At night doth bait his steeds the ocean waves among."

The labors of old Sol, to be sure, are a little out of
the line of the business man, but not so much out of it
that he can afford to disregard the example or declare
that rest and recreation are but snares,

Delusions mere, inventions of the devil,

to bamboozle the thrifty and keep up the world's stock of
drones. If the devil did invent them I have a much
higher opinion of him than usually obtains, and the
proverb is right— the old fellow is "not so black as he's
painted."

What I have recited in the foregoing pages comprises
but a small portion of the very many pleasant and exciting incidents and experiences enjoyed in my tussle with

the wilds of Nature. Though the time was comparatively
short the trips were not. By land and water, by rail,
steamboat, wagon, buckboard, yacht, row boat and birch-
bark canoe, the miles covered were over ten thousand.
No trifling distance; and yet through it all I was never
ill but once, and the damage done then was not serious
enough to prevent my returning home,

> " Full of vigor, tough and glad,
> Feeling like a wiry lad,"

and with a capacity for work that was well worth its cost
of two months time.

And now a parting word to you, you man of business,
chained like a felon in his cell, bereft of sunlight,
harassed with care, tiring your brain over the one mighty
problem of money-making—or else some scheme to stave
off financial disaster—'twill pay you to ponder on my
words and my experience and call a halt. Make up your
mind that money without health is a much greater
calamity than health without money. Leave your desk
and turn your back on the steaming streets of civilization
and your thoughts where Nature tempts with her trout
streams, her mirrored lakes and her game-abounding
retreats; to her forests, fragrant with balsamic odors and
watered by living streams, streams wholesome with the
leechings of the Spruce, and Pine, and Cedar—Nature's
own nectar; a draught of it and you'll need no other
stimulant. Then when the days sport is over and the
night comes, what a revelation is in store for you ! Cud-
dled in your warm sleeping bag, with plenty of blankets,
you "lay me down" on your bed of spruce boughs

whose odors play thick about you, filling the air and soothing you quickly into babe-like slumber. In the morning, spryer than the sun, you leave your bed before him, armed with a double-edged apppetite, so keen and new you wonder where it came from. Trust me for what I tell you, but even my words but faintly speak the novel joys which await you. Once more I say, forget " the shop" and all which that implies, and with the poet Rowe you may exclaim to some purpose:

" Begone my cares! I give you to the winds."

THOMAS MARTINDALE.

www.ingramcontent.com/pod-product-compliance
Lightning Source LLC
Chambersburg PA
CBHW030905050726

47500CB00009B/1052